The Perfect Heart

ALSO BY GEOF HEWITT

Poetry

Hewitt's Guide to Slam Poetry and Poetry Slam
I Think They'll Lay My Egg Tomorrow
Just Worlds
Living in Whales: Vermont Public School Stories & Poems (ed.)
Only What's Imagined
Poem & Other Poems
Quickly Aging Here: Some Poets of the 1970's (ed.)
Selected Poems of Alfred Starr Hamilton (ed.)
Stone Soup
Today You Are My Favorite Poet: Writing Poems with Teenagers
Writing Without Walls: Boise Writing in the Schools (ed. with James Hepworth)

Poems in Performance

The Maple Corner Tape: Poems from Vermont (with Chuck Meese)
DVD included with *Hewitt's Guide to Slam Poetry and Poetry Slam*

Nonfiction

A Portfolio Primer
Working for Yourself

The Perfect Heart

Selected & New Poems

by Geof Hewitt

Mayapple Press 2010

Published by   MAYAPPLE PRESS
                408 N. Lincoln St.
                Bay City, MI 48708
                www.mayapplepress.com

ISBN 978-0932412-92-8

ACKNOWLEDGMENTS

The author is grateful to the following magazines and journals, which first published many of these poems: *Agni Review, Asphalt, Cedar Rock, Chicago Review, Choice, The Colorado Review, Country Journal, Doones, Dragonfly, Epoch, Exquisite Corpse, Foxfire, Green Mountains Review, Harper's, Hearse, Human Voice Quarterly, Hunger Mountain, The Iowa Defender, Lemming, Lillabulero, Negative Capability, New: American and Canadian Poetry, New Letters, The News and the Weather, The North Stone Review, Organic Gardening and Farming, The Paris Review, Poetry Now, Pop Politics.com, The Portsmouth Review, Potato Hill Poetry Newsletter, The Queen City Review, Reading Matters, Rivendell, The Sierra Madre Review, The Spirit that Moves Us, Truck, Willard and Maple.*

"The Gift" and "Seasons" first appeared in *Poem & Other Poems* (The Kumquat Press, 1966). "The Couple Parking on the Motorcycle" first appeared in *Waking Up Still Pickled*, Lillabulero Poetry Pamphlet #3 (Lillabulero Press, 1967). "At the Trumansburg Fair" first appeared as *Kumquat Broadside #7* (The Kumquat Press, 1967). "I Was Gonna Hitch from the Pig Farm," "The Moon," and "Passing Thru" first appeared in *The Corn* (Blue Moon Poetry Pamphlets, Inchelium, WA, 1975). "Comet Come," "Day of Gold," "The Last Words," and "Susan Torrey" first appeared in *I Think They'll Lay My Egg Tomorrow*, Vermont Poetry Chapbook Series (Stinehour Press/Vermont Council on the Arts, 1976). "The Flies" first appeared in *Dear Winter: Poems for the Solstice*, ed. Marie Harris (Northwood Press, 1984). "Bluebird" first appeared in *Heartbeat of New England: An Anthology of Contemporary Nature Poetry*, ed. James Fowler (Tiger Moon Press, 2000). "I'm Back" first appeared in *The Burlington Poetry Slamthology, Volume 1* (The Minimalist Press, 2001). "Harvest, 2001" first appeared in *September 11, 2001: American Writers Respond*, edited by William Heyen (Etruscan Press, 2002). "Lightning Turkey" and "Question" first appeared in *The Burlington Poetry Slamthology, Volume 2* (The Minimalist Press, 2002). "At One With the Blue Night," "February Sequence," and "The Frozen Man" first appeared in *Stone Soup* (Ithaca House, 1974). "Confession," "The Damp October," "Down East," "Fresh Corn," "For Anna," "Recipe," and "Introduction" first appeared in *Just Worlds* (Ithaca House/Greenfield Review Press, 1989). "The Kind of Poetry I Write," "The Viewmaster" (formerly "Stereogram"), "Syllables," "The Sandman," "Delicate," "Edge," "This Is Gross," "Orson," "Just Kidding, Honest," "Leaf Peepers," "Moth," "The Wife Agrees," "Potter," "The Right Words," "The Ultimate Commute," and "Upside Down" first appeared in *Only What's Imagined* (The Kumquat Press, 2000).

Cover photos courtesy of Geof Hewitt and Judy Kerman. Cover designed by Judy Kerman. Book designed and typeset by Amee Schmidt with cover titles in Britannic Bold and poem titles and text in Californian FB. Author photo courtesy of Jeb Wallace-Brodeur.

CONTENTS

1980-1990

FOREWORD

The chance to poke through 45 years of poems has been an enormous gift from the Vermont Arts Council: encouragement-in-dollars. Thank you!

These poems are printed in approximately chronological order, assembled with the hope that readers will scan for something they like, then read the poems around it.

I've attempted to create a format that treats the poems as equals, none favored with a top of the page title, just a running account of 45 years of writing poems. I entered more than 200 poems on my computer, then eliminated enough—harder work than writing and revising them—to offer a collection that will squeeze into your bookshelf or, better, find space near a favorite chair.

Thanks to David, Dana, and Aurora for providing a week of studio space in their Jamestown, NY home, while I selected and entered the 200-plus poems, and to Alex Kanevsky, who courageously reviewed the fat manuscript and graciously helped me determine which poems to cut.

I also want to thank Judith Kerman, Amee Schmidt, and Matthew Falk for their patience and care in the editing and design of this book!

With its title poem, this book is dedicated to Janet.

Geof Hewitt
Calais, VT

1965-1970

SEASONS

Today, you remove it from the freezer,
and the snowball you have saved since March
misses the ice cream truck entirely.

THE GIFT

As if your eyes were really failing
I come to you with this Mother's Day gift:
A glass that lights and magnifies small print
Six times: For phone books, hymns, and greeting cards.
Six times you inspect it, smiling toward me
Thanking thanking and your head shakes. Behind
Your eyes I see my failure, clear as print.

My eyes would hide themselves, but you take
And hold me like a bad son: I've hidden
Long within dark caves, the dark caves of your
Body, caverns of solid love:
       My tongue is a bat:
The old apologies
       are breaking from my mouth.

Was I as big a burden just before
I cracked through you with my head to gasp first air?
Was my first cry our final time together?
Have I like old eyes failed you since that breath?

EMERGENCY AT EIGHT

Across the street, my aunt has lost
    her baby: for nearly as long
    as I can think back, we've had to be
So careful with her: no games at all
    for one thing and brush by her
    in tight corners without even touching
That wall of stomach, breakable as some new egg.

But now the sirens have died in my ears
    like adult voices, come and gone
    and taken her: she'll have to stay
Away awhile, getting better
    and forgetting all the work she wasted:
    holding eight months my broken cousin.
My house is quiet at this time. My mother holds the phone.

AT THE TRUMANSBURG FAIR

We didn't miss a thing, but saw
every booth: the place where fifteen
cents can buy a cherry apple,
the spot where only men can go
(heads down, quickly: BURLEY-Q:
"Come in, boys, if you're not scared,
see what we have on hand").

Rita O'Donnell came to mind at the penny
pitch: years ago, I'd lost her to another
boy—one who *could* win her
a squeaking bear. You laughed as I tried
still again to get a penny
into the dish. Really, I was distracted
by the dressed-up farm boys
and a girl whose hands were sticky with cotton
candy, whose breasts were just beginning
to show beneath her dress.

The Demolition Derby
featured drivers from all over
the state: proud as fathers, they swung
into their old wrecks, cars picked
clean of upholstery and chrome,
skulls of old vacations, maybe Xmas
presents of another year. The crowd
roared stupidly with you and me as spotlights
nailed the smoky air and metal bent:
(a woman next to you was grunting
as if she were one of the cars).

The whole ride home I thought of making love,
of kissing your candy apple lips
while watching that Dream Girl competition
they have on tv: when I told you this you smiled,
amused for the first time all day.
And when we got home, I stripped you faster
than cars can destroy one another, left marks
on your neck and arms, persuaded you to stay
the night. Then I dreamed that we were still
at the fair, watching our children
in the ferris wheel, high against the moon.

NOVEMBER, 1966

Years were going to lend
objectivity,
make possible some expression
other than the lowered eyes,
dark cloth on certain days.
Or flowers on the grave.

Janitors who raise the flags can control a city
merely by doing half the job:
once one was fired a week after
        his wife died: he'd thrown
        half a population into mourning.

At funerals there's always the cars:
        Cadillacs in tandem, lights
        blazing like electric suns.
Different Cadillacs
honk incessant horns.

We are,
        after all,
                for show:
                        share my
                                sorrow, take a piece
of my joy. Our smiles, our own sad
                                stories
                        told at bars
                or at church
        reveal
that fact.

Nothing is more final than the fact.
There is nothing final about what the fact starts.
A president drops and pens start moving.

        NEIGHBOR

The stranger in the next
apartment rattles
in her bed at night and moans:
I hear her with my whole ear
        pressed against the wall
        we share
        from private sides: I'd like to
        call her on the telephone:

"Hello.
        This is your next-
apartment neighbor speaking!
I heard your bed last night and thought
I'd ask you in for something, I'll give
you tea or beer, just name your

poison." CLICK:
she's hung up on me.

       Or I could go and knock and say
       (as if she doesn't know)
just who I am and what I want.

We're not such strangers after all
that she's not heard me arched in bed
in dreams:
The wall between us turns to glass
and bodies fill our sounds.

THE COUPLE PARKING ON THE MOTORCYCLE

Up the street, as if to tease
Me, a car with headlights
Ekes forward, thin beams
Coming closer to the couple
Parking on the motorcycle:

I lean from my 3rd story
With eyes as glassy as a window
Straining at the dark:

Love on a motorcycle! How grand
To have a girl so supple,
So open to the call of April streets
That she can relax on triangular seats
Lean back and offer you herself,
Legs smooth as handlebars under the chromium moon.

How often love could catch you balanced
In the windy night, rev you
Like a captive engine screaming
To have its clutch let out,

If not for those damned headlights, drawing closer.

11

WAKING UP STILL PICKLED

This room's become the Baltimore
Zoo: my head is a cage where thoughts
rattle the bars and stalk
like rugged bears, dying
for exercise: both of me crowds to watch.

My jacket, wounded dog, lies where it
fell last
night, one broken arm bent
under it: it whines to be hung up,
its button eyes me from the floor—
boneless sack of cheap cloth needs me

but will conform to anything. It has no will
save what I give it:
bulges with my belly, grows
hot precisely when I do and sweats.

My pants have taken another
tack, preserve their press from the nail
above my bed: cuffs threaten down at me
like two dry elephant trunks, juxtaposed.

Preserve me if I die from drinking—
o stuff me like a rare ape
and dress me only in those clothes
that need me and become.

LETTER TO HIS WIFE

Lately I walk without a cane,
my legs are stiff but that remains
consideration
hardly worth the trouble of your thought.
> I remember once when we were
> young, how we could laugh at older
> couples, their determined optimism:
> polio shots at sixty-five!

I would not have troubled you
so late in life, if you had not been
my wife once and if I didn't feel
a need, some need that cripples
me at times like numb fingers,
withering legs: my cook is good,
she makes the broth at midday, the nurse considerate
and friendly as a volunteer.

   Last spring I had a fall
   (I think it was the cane
   that jinxed me) and since
   I've had to keep a nurse.

I hope you understand: there really
is no reason for my calling you
this way, unless it be that just
once more I'd like to feel
your sullen enmity: perhaps
if you ignore me now, I can be
satisfied again, I'll feel as if
your love for me still turns in you
like hatred stored for years:
the way you severed all your ties
with me, this town, our friends,
was in its way a consolation.

   A letter came for you last year
   I opened by mistake.
   After so long
   one rarely checks the name.

Perhaps you've wondered what would come
of it if you returned. Oh, not for long
—I know your feelings there—
but just for, say, a week,
ten days. I'd give the nurse some time
off, she really only serves to talk
now that I'm walking well again:
I'd light a fire each day you stayed.
There might not be much to talk about,
unless you feel yourself again and want
to bring back those old arguments.

I know I'll never win. That's half the fun.
     Before I close just let me say
     how beautiful this winter is.
     I have a room where you could
     sleep, first floor, no stairs to climb.
     The snow has nearly buried the old shed
     twice this November, every night is dead
     quiet. Because the dogs are gone,
     I sleep without those ear plugs now.

LOVE POEM

you fell   the sharp curb cut your skin
we were already late
we had been quarreling all day   you
said it doesn't hurt   I pretended
to believe you   you said I'm so sorry
come on we'll be late   you said
I hope there wasn't an early KO   I
booed with the crowd the 5th round on
we fought the crowd back to the car
getting change for the tollbooth   I
saw the bone beneath your blood
and lights reflected on your face

THANKSGIVING

1.
Mist from the north
and trees have dropped leaves,
heavy with color, to their roots.

Wrinkles in the ceiling,
timbers sagging like the places
where his face could almost stretch

through skin. Things crack
in cold weather
unless an inner warmth

breathes through to meet the wind.
A tree was warped into this house
that every year needs jacking up,

a thousand thoughtless nails
struck here and there
to keep it standing.

I watch a cat work through the leaves.

2.
Only if you were patient
could you kill ducks
by aiming at the moon:

I was young & believed
what he said & so I never killed
a duck, in the breeze the

moon's dazzle
breaking to pieces
on strands of his hair.

THE FROZEN MAN

A new disease waltzing in his bones
    and good doctors consulted whose frank
        voices made it plain he couldn't be cured
            within that century,

he rented locker space and told his family slowly
    that, to numb the pain and as a contribution
        to scientific knowledge, he'd be frozen
            solid for a hundred years.

The children were too young to understand, his wife
    (who realized now she'd never known

him anyway) had long since been resigned
   to his strange ideas

and kissed him hard before he entered
   the preparation room, promising
      she'd raise the boys, reminding them to tell
         their sons to take him out

one day. Then, naked as water in a tray,
   he shut his eyes before they froze, his heart
      was closing down over the thick blood,
         his mind was stopping: there was

no pain. His hearing lasted longest and the voices
   of the observation room faded almost into
      jagged colors. "Relax," they said. And,
         as he felt himself go hard:

"Try not to shiver."

Little happened in the hundred years:
   his wife told his sons to tell their sons
      to have him thawed, and doctors did, indeed,
         find a cure for his disease.

And when, in 2068, they rolled him out,
   applying heat, he wakened to the shivers
      that had rocked him into sleep, and met
         his children's children, happy

to see him looking so good. He noticed
   quickly that their smiles were like the grins
      that might be used by a race that's rid itself
         of death but not of hunger.

And the eyes that he saw were calm, unquestioning,
   as if all answers, like TV dinners,
      lie warmed on a plate and waiting
         to be probed by hasty forks.

TOD VAN ALLEN'S PISSING MATCH

From the cliff at bedtime just before
  he put them in their sacks
the counselor would get the little campers to piss:
  he who hits the birch from here
    gets coffee for breakfast—or all
      the cocoa he can drink!

The stunt was easy and it got the little guys
  relaxed before the sleeping bag
would pull them into its seductive warmth.

Little Tod was worst of the lot,
  with important relatives so even if he was
just five years old he got to be a camper too.
  They'd called him "Turtle" secretly,
    the whole climb long, he'd slip
      and the weight of his pack

would glue him to the trail,
arms and legs working the air.

Tom and Jim, the twins, had been on camping trips before
  and took their marks and one near
reached the birch with his brave stream.
  Two more campers made game tries and
    the counselor, who hadn't pissed all day,
      of course,

made the tree and even got his stream
to reach the second branch.

Tod had fallen behind and reached the group
  too late to see who held what mark.
"Hit the tree" was all they chanted
—not unkindly, for this is not a story
  of revenge but strength—
    and he leaned back, unzipped
and calmly took aim. A flash
of urine spurted out and climbed

the white bark
  limb after limb
until he was done.
  Tod led the whole group
    back to camp and shared the morning coffee
      with his mates.

DECEMBER 31, 1969

With a net I chased the butterfly
And eased it past the others
Into a Mason jar, which
Neither caught their magic
Nor grew heavier.

Tonight the profits of a decade
Clog at the tip, no word
Can catch the flight of years.
A decade flips easy, nothing
Seems to end or to begin.
A president was killed and I
Got schooled, I saw men walking
On the moon and was not glad.

None of me seems different
From the boy, engaged
In stealing butterflies,
None of me is bigger than
The boy who angles through my mind
To bring his small collection home.

1970-1980

THE DISAPPOINTMENT

I could come to you
For strength, they said
I'd find you

Quiet, sad
& bent as if
To carry something broken

Just inside the skin.
You've shed the smile
They said you drank the pain

Of every generation:
It gives you life, the way the
Gasoline destroys its engine.

What made *you* so special anyway?
Even fleas could find a home on you,
Tickling the body that shrinks

Each day, scouring flesh
To find a final meal:
I watch the numbers grow

I see the food get scarce
I hear the tempers flare.
I see you in the center

Giving all you've got.

A DELICACY

This morning for breakfast I had honey-covered ants.
Tasted like honey with ants in it.

MY MARTIAN GIRLFRIEND

People brag about girls with green eyes.
She had legs like blades of grass.
They drifted up & over my body.
She'd float me to a place
& show me how she'd trained fire
to walk the length of her skin,

her face making change after change.
"It hurts but I love it,"
she said when it
licked between blades.
Martians feel pain but don't burn.
If I tortured her she laughed:
I carved her with my knife but her wounds
turned into smiles. I made extra mouths

for her and she kissed my whole body.
When my feet hurt, she could stretch out a stomach
for them to walk in, easing their cramps.
But the Martian girl has gone.
Like a curtain moving from its shadow,
as if to float back in the absence of wind,
she drifted up.
She sang but I could not move:

Come with me now my earth boyfriend
& we can be lovers forever
& no one will know
& it will not matter.

DAY OF GOLD

We walked the foothills talking
of water—its miracle on the rocks
each spring, its shimmer down gullies
of its own path's choice. Earlier
on the rickety swinging bridge
that sags all but into Grimes Creek I lost

my sense of balance: mistakenly focused
on the speeding melted snow beneath.
"Don't be afraid to crawl!" my host cried out,
then: "Dignity on hands and knees
upon this bridge can be maintained." Foot by foot
I inched my way from slab to slab.

Even seedlings have it rough getting started here.
The Idaho summer is nearly rainproof and these
plastic snakes are necessary.
They siphon it over a ridge
from a mysterious cave
with an underground pool that's never gone dry.
Old Olai, who homesteaded this land,
used to have a still in there.
We looked for antlers and gold,
finding little of either. My hands sifted
the gravel and Bette said
"fool's gold just shines. The real stuff's dull

until you spit on it." I spat and watched
my rocks refuse to shine,
unlike the sun! What fools to scrape
the earth for wealth in this or any weather!
This country is so beautiful, the hills roll easily
until the mountains actually begin:
we tried to walk it softly
to miss the early flowers with our feet
but stooping now and then
to break one from the ground, crumble it
& sniff. This is sorrel—Bette Joy's sorrel.
Hens & chickens survive on rock, and in a gully where I hoped

for gold, I dug up a horsetail. Listen for the rock chuck's cheep,
the Indian loves him but the white man kills
for sport. Approaching the ledge of a gigantic cliff
we saw where someone had a couple
sixes of Pabst. Too many to carry off.
Humans can't accept mortality. They leave mementoes:
forests planted or "improved."
The hand has dipped too deep and now we want

to grow it back. In 1909 this hill was rich
with softwood. Then in 1910 the clear cut came
and now between the tiny seedlings
set out by the Joys, alfalfa soothes the land.

The buttercup—earth's oldest flower.
Golden willows there in Nancy's yard,
basket of gold as we walked into her cabin,
out, temporarily, of the sun.

And now, returning late, the mountains
all fall far and smooth in shadow. As we pass at 55
deer come from the remaining woods
to graze in this last hour of light.

AT ONE WITH THE BLUE NIGHT

Cramped like thoughts in a brain,
We're knees up, dinner through a tube,
We're partners whirling, floating skins
Inside our weighted suits.

And now, as the world watches,
You want out. I distract you with Mars, I drip
The dream-juice through your tube
And sleep you past the final station.

A galaxy creeps by the glass,
Our breath becomes ice, we
Breathe it back. I watch as you develop
Gills, an aluminum grill.

You want to touch
But even if your gloves came off I wouldn't feel
Your fingers through my leather health: your grip,
Persuasion to turn around or somehow

Get older! This isn't the ship they wanted to build,
One of your knees floats by, obsolete,

The other—no! that one's mine: our waists
Are shrinking—we grow into smaller bodies

Like tadpoles, until just weightlessness fills our suits.
And you are a child
Standing for the first time, curious
How you got there, amazed by your height.

We are learning how young we can be when memory
Conks out: I am forgetting to stay in my suit:
Already naked, you have floated through the feed-tube.
Even years apart, we travel nowhere together.

BEN WRESTLES THE DEMON

Where his eyes focus, somewhere between my shoulder and the wall,
where they can reach no farther in the air, he sees and watches some-
thing, afraid. His arms and hands jaggle and his face contorts as if the
thing is on him.

What he wrestles may be the knowledge that he is, like his eyes, aimed
at some invisible point. And the most important thing he'll ever know,
he's far too young to remember.

IN LIKE A LION

The white howl of March
Sweeps down from Canada.
A glove is frozen to the spade.
The rope holds a defiant curve,

It smiles at gravity.
I stamp out your name in the snow
So big great altitude is needed to read.
And, "I am a lonely secret

Like pajamas stuffed with pillowcases."
How yesterday's sunshine made me feel

I'd got to spring scot-free,
How lovely to hear it come through branches

Through open window like a voice you love
Says let's dance.

ANOTHER NUTTY DREAM

Uncle Phil forgives me for the time Dan
puked in the back seat
and asks if I want to drive his Cadillac:
"She's okay, but maybe not good enough for you,"
he whistles, his moustache no wider
than a politician's eyebrow.

He plucks another car from his repertoire
& I'm on the Garden State
shifting gears like mad, a row
of dependent faces peering from behind.

The dots on the asphalt
are useless by the time they're beneath us
and the car turns into stained glass;
choirs are warming up on scales.

If I could wake I'd be glad to own nothing.

THE FLOOD

Mother said the dogs would know by instinct
        what to do, I wasn't going to cry.
Chunks of house rolled in the froth and I saw
        Philip Decker's dart board, made a stab
and almost tipped the boat, my mother screamed
        and Edward was already crying.

Father told the men he wouldn't leave
        but when the water broke
the porch he rowed across the yard

to check on Mrs. James. Her house
was there but she was gone, he said
her son had come.

He boated right into the living room
where Mother had us on the table.
He said, "Get in,"
and Mother let me down, then Edward
and herself. He steadied us
by holding to the couch.

Blackie was upstairs barking down
and Lady'd disappeared.
That's when Mother told me about instinct.
Father didn't say a word but kept on rowing.
We were going nowhere,
we were staying up.

He rowed uphill to Church Street
where the buildings eighty years before
had held the people when their homes
wept out to the brown Atlantic.
A nurse made soup for us, we stayed three days
and I met neighbors I didn't know we had.

Then for the next two summers
Father patched the house.

SHUDDER

Say at the end of the day you return to discover
she's packed and gone, taken the baby
and your car, the cash, all liquor and jewelry.
She has left only the dog!

For months there were hints she was disenchanted:
the banana peel in the bathtub, a roller
skate balanced on the ladder rung
while you repaired the roof of your now-empty

man you've earned the right to shudder
tears came easily before
and "nervous breakdowns" are so common

                                                             so go on,
                                              get it on,
                       let your system
            break into that
helpless gasp,

that shudder dealt by bones.

SHUDDER #2

What if the cruelest Monster catches you
Messing with his wife & then observes
A curious likeness in you to his only son,
The idiot he's supported all these years?

His wife, a tasty quiff no less ugly
In her meaner moods than he, decides
To goad him on & throws her naked body
Between yours and his advancing hulk:

"Beware: do not harm the father of your son,"
She hisses as he lunges for her.
What he will do when he finishes her
You'd like to know

But you've a rendezvous to keep
& miles to go before you sleep

THE QUINCY 1972 JUKEBOX FANTASY WALTZ

"Just like the war,"
he says. "Always rained something: bombs in
clear weather," and toys the beer glass through a
semi-circle of its sweat, thumbs the label in

half of his Budweiser bottle. Except for him
no one's talking: half a dozen regulars stare
at their drinks and haven't listened to a word.

The television's big glass eyelid
opens up, a voice
yells: Turn it up—

in disbelief
the heartbeat doubles for an instant, triples.
Then feels the drag of gravity.

3 parachutes appear like clouds
whitened by the sun's escape
from shadow

harness and life raft
the chopper waits
to lift the brittle men.

He mumbles: "Fuckin' Navy," someone 4 stools down wants to punch
him for his noise. Before this can happen they are reminded by the bar-
keep that we're all good patriots. Someone buys a round. We pass the
time. Someone wonders who's our greatest patriot and Navy and Army
weave past each other, out the door. The cueball clicks the fourteen off.
New channel brings a documentary on the poor. I slip back into the
room & let my jukebox fantasy's ragtime rhythms weave a silk scream
bubble, got to line up, listen to the news:

There is a little place in Heaven
where is kept for you until you die
everything you treasured & lost as a child,
everything you lost & later treasured as a man:
it is the place where friends await
hearts of forgiveness, the cruel ways you were
at times, the ring that glows in the dark
lost behind the Chrysler's back seat

2 days before your father sold it:
you know, the place of memories

& time to enjoy them forever
forever time enough & friends enough

how nice mind's eye   can take you there

FEBRUARY SEQUENCE

1.
Dawn with its eyelid of song
sashays in
to nudge sleep's elbow

& you waken with a dream, sleep's energy,
the unborn child, trapped in your skull,
that funnybone

waken to the snow & a wicker rocking chair
tipped over by wind, first sunlight, first realshine
in three weeks:

shadows, startling shadows and the apple tree
too stiff to shrug, holds its awkward leafless
haywire dancing pose

how steady from harvest
till spring
that frozen pregnancy

(January thaw got some wise acre's maples
excited & he tapped them & word's out he may
be the richest sugar maker this year)

2.
A funny thing happened. We had to wait to use the telephones, too
many of us and not enough phones: they had some lieutenants making
the connections and they'd call us into the room when our turn came.
The Colonel came and called my name and I heard Joanelle's voice and
she said, "How are you feeling, Honey?" and I said, "I'm okay. Baby I
love you." She said, "I can't believe it's really you." A lieutenant tapped

me on the shoulder. I had the wrong telephone. I was being welcomed by another man's wife. It was very strange.

3.

How simply the movement of my own vision resembles that of every bird, every skyscraper and rock—each bouncing swirl of molecule, the tiny margin of circumstance that keeps me from being a bird or skyscraper or rock. If I do not visit the stars, do not journey below my feet, I don't sustain the glitter of snow scattered by the chickadee's wing.

Mind each step a baby takes, rehearsal
for a dance, each sound from which
he'll learn to make & choose words,
each bite that becomes body or energy or thought,
or never mind such obvious building of experience,
think instead of arrangements
of molecules learning his habits
becoming him, they pile up and say hi.

THE BIRD

You said we had a bird
caught in the smoke pipe.
The flashlight showed a puff of black feathers
so small we knew it couldn't survive outdoors
unless its mother came.

We tried to fish it out, you screamed
when it fluttered against your hand
(my arm too fat to squeeze down
the pipe—you'd have to be the hero)
so we decided that, with the stove poker,

I'd give the bird a turn
until its eyes reflected up the flashlight's beam.

And it came busting out through soot
blind or dazed
by the miraculous opening,

lit out of that stovepipe and waited
while I cupped my hands around it

and you looked for the cat to restrain.
The bird, so calm, as if it sensed
its final chance was trusting the finger
of man, blinked & hunched
sooty down in my hand,

thinking, I think, its suffering days was done
& flew
    surprise
        cartwheels in the sky
around the house one time & higher

crazy, free, & motherless
that con bird old enough to find its worms alone,
the bird of rocking paradise careening from the dark.

DID YOU KNOW

that, watching you walk from the house
past the mailbox, down the hot, dirt road

I saw you grow smaller and less clear
until at times the dust of passing cars
made you impossible to see at all

and when I said I wasn't watching you
is that because, as at the moment of your nightmare,
when your voice's heaving woke the house,
I hoped you'd never know we knew, we heard
the screams and had to waken you?

I know that cries for help can go unanswered,
the way a head tilts back to take a drink,
exposing throat, so white and fine . . .

I can't tell when you choose to listen.
Or if, like me, you never hear the words
as fully as the sound of someone's voice,
the noise that never lies,
then I know you knew, for instance, I *was* watching.

You could hear the quaking air dragged from the gut
to lie, and earlier you'd felt the youngster's eye-beams
hone through dust. It doesn't work that way
with memories and time, but yes the years do cast
their own dim veil, the writing penciled in begins to fade . . .

And when I'm walking on that road I feel the wind
melt my eyes, peculiar how it turns them red and small into water.

I feel your lifelessness already, these wretched last years
sentenced you, and wonder if these lines
can ever make the long trip out of me and into you.

PASSING THRU

You see them at truckstops, signs that litter the walls,
Work fascinates me I can sit & watch it for hours, Plan Ahea,
And the waitress so sullen you want to tip extra just to show her
How wrong she was about you, her white dress with little bumps
All over the material making it look almost gray and you see thru
To the bra doing its thin job and she wants you to pay up
So she can go home, saunters over and yawns between chews "You thru?"
And not to be mean but because you're lonely you ask for another donut:
She extends it with aluminum pincers so it seems germproof
But you watched earlier when she emptied the bakery cellophane
Damn near fondling each one
As if here at least was something she cared for
And licking all the extra sugar off her fingers at the end.

"To hell with aluminum—let's dance!" you cry and twist her hand
Over the counter so she drops pincers and your donut
"Hey cut that out—whatsa matter with you you crazy or somethin: Joe!"
And she starts yelling but you've already passed thru
That critical tunnel where you decide:

"This is a dream, I'll do what I please."
And one of the truckers looks up from the coffee he stirred with his eyes
As you think of your mother who told you about them and how one
       would kill you someday just like they got your father

And you dance with her back and forth over the countertop
Until Joe comes out at which point the trucker gets involved too
And both of them have you by the legs and the waitress is saying
"Wise guy wise guy" over and over
And the donut and the pincers are on the floor
And if you wanna know more go do it yourself

EAGLE ROCK

Remember us to Eagle Rock
Billy Koenig & me at 9 years apiece
hiking one Saturday in early May
way up past the house with half a pack
of embezzled cigarettes & enough matches
to light each one a dozen times,

Remember us to Eagle Rock
where couples in their cars
pulled off the road to watch the N.Y. skyline
& make love as Billy & me
dizzy from tobacco sitting on the big pavilion
of the castle with its stoned out windows
wondering what to do once we felt better

And how as if we had no choice
we'd find ourselves each time
working toward the place the cars were parked
provided by the town, a pressure seal
for lovers prevented by circumstance
from doing it at home

And picture Koenig & me, pockets stuffed
with newly sprouted acorns
we used to stone the lovers

taking such liberties with our health
& how when we did get chased

we'd run & run & run
half laughing and half very scared
some wild-yelling cursing half-dressed
passion victim in pursuit
I hated to trip but often did
Billy usually way ahead of me, down down
to a cave we knew where
we'd heave & choke & get our breath,
lungs aching from the cigarettes & from the chase
& laugh & swear we'd never come so close
to getting caught.

THE DAISY

It was only a Daisy,
the kind sold by coupon off the backs of comic books:
Gee Dad it's a Daisy! he grins up at his father
from the package where—cradled like Jesus—lies the gun.
You can tell he's sincere and when the father's around
he merits the gun and carries it properly
never taking aim unless he seriously intends to shoot.
But one day dad goes to work and he can relax
so he sights in a squirrel, then panics as its gray heaving
slows at his feet: he pumps BB after BB through the eye,
each incomplete thud of the airgun
taking him further into his decision to end its suffering.

He forgets how painful killing was
within a year and he and Schulzy
take the Daisy down and grease her up
and go out on the prowl, first that glittering globe
—a basketball sized Xmas-like thing—
kept by some rich people on a concrete pedestal.
They crouch among the rhododendron leaves, he remembers
with satisfaction how it rose with a poof
and held its shape, briefly enlarged,
before collapsing, shattered, in a joyful tinkle

off its stand. Even as an adult
he drives that street and observes the pedestal, empty.

What is it—two Saturdays—before they tire
of things and decide moving targets would be better?
And then almost floats into view
the new neighbors' kid pedaling his fat ass
along South Mountain Avenue, almost too far
to hit with BBs for sure, so they sight him in
& pump off maybe half a dozen each, Schulz
screaming cowboy style at the end running toward the road
waving the gun like a flag.
The kid, by now, is standing in the pedals,
his ass ballooning out behind him up & down,
and Schulzy slows and takes his final aim.

2 hours later they see a cop car in his father's driveway
and decide to unscrew the barrel and hide all their BBs
then run outside dipping muzzle into earth
and airpoof it around in clear sight of the law,
two innocent kids who, by circumstance, happened to be playing
with a harmless gun when Fat Ass was wounded.
But the cop breaks their story fast,
the one gun that was used is their Daisy.

Was it he or Schulz fired the shot
that made such a terrible bruise on the Markly boy's buttock?
Apologies heave up their throats throughout the confession
and the gun, at last, is taken away.

SUSAN TORREY

When I think of early sex I think of Susan Torrey.
She was, at 12, a year my senior
but her father'd been transferred so much
she was put in my grade when she came to our school.
Not only that but she moved into a house across the street!
Only one thing wrong with Susan was her aunt,
Miss Reed, who was thin and seemed short to me then,

so looking back I'd say she was probably 100 pounds,
5 feet tall, and a gray 45. So unloved
if anyone had lain with her he'd've snapped her in half,
like a twig in March.
Miss Reed was *mean* and it was one of those situations
where even in 6th grade you wondered
"If someone could love her would she change?"

Susan's mother was fine & so was her father.
They were both just fat enough to know a good time.
Susan and I would "make out."
Brenda Lee's "Sweet Nothins" was big
on Hit Parade and if you want to know
our scene the summer of '54 just listen
to that song:
       Mama comes to the porch, turns on the front light
       Says "come on in darlin, that's enough for tonight."
       Sweet Nothins . . .
Miss Reed would come out next if Susan didn't send me home,
so the first warning was sufficient to stay our smooching.
I gave Susan an ID bracelet with my name (first & last) engraved.
"This doesn't mean we're going steady," I promised.

We were watching the World Series on Susan Torrey's father's
TV that September or October
when Willie Mays made that fantastic over the shoulder
football-like catch in center field that robbed
Vic Wertz of the winning homer.
I was in the bathroom when it happened.
Miss Reed was on the couch knitting and Mr. Torrey
just looked up when I came in and said
"You'll never guess what you just missed!"

I bought an old hearing aid
and was trying it out under the red beech
on our front lawn, talking into the unit
with the earplug jammed into my ear.
I remember distinctly I was saying, "Testing. Testing."
and "Shit. Shit." alternately
when suddenly I knew someone was looking
over my shoulder from behind the tree.

I was embarrassed but that wasn't anything new
with Susan Torrey. We did a lot of embarrassing things
together. We played spin the bottle. We kissed
any other time we got the chance and I remember
thinking our lips pressed together felt like worms.
But it was fun, especially trying not to get caught.
And she let me feel her breasts
through the gray sweater Miss Reed had knitted.

Susan's married now and "just beautiful"
according to my mother who's got terrific taste.
She came in the driveway about 5 years ago
just after I'd graduated from graduate school:
I was off in Hawaii teaching. She had a child
or 2 with her then & drove a Country Squire.
I bless her now and all my childhood friends
and curse the strange fears that keep us apart.

LIQUIDS

Coffee wakes you from that sleep-bruised face,
fraggles your nerves
till they push you out into the day, into the twitch.

Rain and dandruff slush creep through your boots,
feet seep. By noon you're ready
to swallow a Pepsi, it sparkles your throat
and in the new sun your sweat bakes as mud turns to dust
on your face. By 5 the excuse to stop: the whistle
runs through your ears, cuts a string in your head.

You become friends with the guy next to you
and agree to stop for a drink. The beer drags the day's crust down,
coats a glistening path and

in the corner of your eye, like the last thought before sleep,
something glints.
It reminds you   something   you can't remember.

A woman with pale powdered breasts and spots on her neck
nurses a brandy alexander and you buy her one.
Your friend from work has excused himself

till morning. He's got family, kids,
and each of you would trade places.
He could love the pale powdered darkness

and the chance to get lushed now and then
and you'd drink all those quarts of non fat milk
just to get close to his wife.

IN SADNESS

In sadness I started for a place
I had hoped to avoid,
a place I'd branched away from
ten years earlier and had to re-track.

Ten years of backtracking I hated myself
for the twenty years I had wasted,
until at the source of my sadness
I realized the only years wasted

were those spent hating myself.
Loving myself for that discovery,
I forgave the years spent hating.
Blithering proud I started down

the same wrong path again.

ELM

Big George came to see the old elm fall,
He's got a nickel says she's
"A hunnert-fifty years at least"
But no one wants to count the rings with George.

Balanced over the notch and a too-low backcut,
The tree is held off the house by its hinge
And a rope coiled around its house-most limb
Then casually hitched to the huge flatbed truck, precaution

Turned necessity. This mammoth truck had
Brought a crane that kept the highest limbs
From crashing loose as the operator's boy dangled
Like a monkey, cutting quickly, proving himself

Ignorant of fear. Maybe 6, maybe 8 full cords
From that operation alone;
The boy swills a beer, his specialty used,
Leans against the idling crane.

Now two saws work the undercut,
Weaken the hinge with the flatbed revved
In the direction the tree must fall.
These guys know what they're doin' predicts George,

Who is right more than half the time.
I got a nickel says the house won't get hit.
No one wants to bet though, even when that elm
Starts shaking back and forth, big truck digging dirt,

George's eyes bulging, his mouth a-stutter,
The qualified cutters scattered,
One saw on fire,
The house placid, rope lashing

Elm, reputations, lives, a house in balance,
Everything is on the line and whomp
Down comes crashing, we measured the stump,
More than 6 feet in diameter of elm.

WEALTH

George flags me down, he needs a ride
to Farnham's place, the millionaire
who bought a farmhouse George is paid to fix.

George would have torn the whole thing down
and started over. "Glad I'm not rich,"
he says. "It makes you get odd."

Farnham is the eldest heir
controlled by trustees who mete his money
only on approval, and his new house

in the country is a project they really like.
For George, this decision in Montreal
means economic boomtimes, reminding him

of his old boss in South Carolina, a lady
of 84 years with a longing to be alone
in a mansion George was always fixing.

She was particular
and when she didn't like the color
of a new-painted room, George painted it over

in the same color and she was extremely pleased.
Another time they looked at concrete
in the hot morning and saw the waves

of heat pouring off it: "Pretty wavy,"
someone complained. "Come back tonight,"
said George, "I'll put the grinder to it"

then spent the day hooking catfish.
About 4:30 the lady's supervisors returned
praising the flatness George's grinder had created.

"'We'll remember that when you get your check,'
and that means I go an extra hundred,"
chortles George, his jowls bouncing.

By now we are at Farnham's and George,
determined to give his morning to talk,
eyes the car door with dread, teases the handle

and points out the features of his job,
a manure pile that he moved 3 times,
"gets frustrating. There's boards

laid horizontal you could jump through.
He didn't want them vertical,
so we had to do it over. Now he's pleased,

says I can borrow his car anytime
but I'm not gonna touch it!
He's a lawyer, he could tie me up for years."

By now I've shut the engine off and waited
through a story, then cleared my throat
and started the engine again,

and George is about to light a cigarette.
He finds the matches with startling ease, lifting
his weight to allow a hand in his pocket,

then settles back reminded of his father,
easy to live with until he caught up with his debts
then got a bit ahead and then what a pain

in the ass. George was the oldest son
and once when a grain shipment
came out a ton short the old man

raved and when he stomped out to find a lawyer
George phoned up to the plant in Deposit, N.Y.,
where they'd already spotted the error

and credited the account. George flicks an ash
neatly into the dashboard ashtray,
lets out a couple lungsful of smoke,

"the lawyer and I agreed privately
to drop the matter, and my father went around
saying, "See, it always pays to get a lawyer.""

Then, in triumph heaving from the car seat
through the door, he turns and issues me a final wink.
"That advice, as you can see, is being taken here."

OFF THE LAND

Dear Will farmed it till he died
and lived with the widow, his daughter.
He was tall and painfully slow.
"You need even the small stones to build a fence,"

he said when the state closed his sawmill
for safety. He worked the only way permitted,
alone: So long as there's no help involved
you can saw your hands off, it said in effect.

Is it Will's brothers or his sons who inherited
the land they never farmed? The forests,
combed and spared. Wasn't Will ever tempted
to cut the whole stand, or take one or two

of those extraordinary hemlocks?
Or maybe he did, in thinning, find the best wood.
What came when he died was his heirs
splitting the take: a big logging operation

clear cut the woods
and a realtor dumped the stripped land
shortly thereafter in ten acre lots.
The house and millpond sold to a young engineer.

Will's gone. But I got a friend
to interview him and Scott wrote a song:
"Old Will Johnson died last year"
is how it starts out. I'm sad

when I think of how Will started
and look at my son who at four
likes air travel. I gape at my garden
remembering Will's, the missing links between us.

CHICKENS

And aren't those baby chicks
creatures of my acquiescence
letting a particularly broody banty hen
have some eggs to set?

Now she acts as if they're completely her
creation, even the rooster has to sneak
blessings to his heirs, and I
get pecked for coming near.

Those chicks get down under her belly
and stay warm in that darkness,
sputtling over each other in morning
when I remove the raincoat
from their cage, the limits of their world
so far. I make their day begin
by letting sunlight in, and feed & water them.
They peek out from underneath

their banty's feathered underside and peep:
"Hey that's Him! I saw God's hand unveiling day!"
And I sit here, twelve hours later, August 26
8:30 p.m. Already the sun is down.

Yeah, winter's coming.
Darkness—God!—I hate to see it come.

BEN CARRIES THE CRACKED EGG

This one's for you Geof
I think they'll lay my egg tomorrow

I WAS GONNA HITCH FROM THE PIG FARM

the whole way
but up to my ankles in pigshit decided
to drive my geriatric Beetle one more trip.

It wheezed and squealed up the shortcut
through the Notch and wobbled, rolling fast,
down through Stowe and something thunked
    & a wheel wouldn't roll by Waterbury
    right in front of the Mobil station where—
    2 years ago—hello John Chambers Mobil, hi!—
we were towed with an engine blown. Thirty dollar tow job.
My jaunty, rusted-out green, dying bug
    clugged into the station too early for anyone
    to be there. I left a note Dear John,
    it said, John the front left hub was smoking &
    thunks I'll call you from Barre

    and a man who works part-time with a chest so hairy
    he had to keep his shirt open to the navel just to give
    the bulge a place to go drove me to the Barre turnoff
—he had an 8 foot pram lashed to the roof
of his wagon & a full-sized harpoon in the bed
"Some trips a man must make alone," he said
    and I retained my tactful cool, envisioned his grimace
    into the teeth of salt waves whipping the boat,
    "Nantucket Sleigh Ride" the harpoon struck home in an offshore
oil whale sperm bank, the line paid out, and the man from Vermont
makes his trip alone, across the Atlantic
towed by blubber & mighty hungry in the end.
    Later I closed the door in the chairwoman's face:
    it pushed her glasses to the side. We laughed.
    She'd been saying: "Your check may come a little late . . ."

    and two Honor Girls drove me straight
    to Plainfield for my interview:
    "I certainly do enjoy poetry,"

I remarked. "Mr. Hewitt, you get high?" she was turned
from the passenger seat with brown pools and a small sack
of hashish by surprise. "You want a little hit?"
    The Honors Taxi! Hashish, pigshit, I figured the 2
    might mingle, but said (clearing the throat) uh . . . not this time
    want to be clear-headed for my meeting;
Cheerist! The things we pass up
in the name of clarity, those brown hashish eyes
but please the Committee if you please, read me any way

that pleases you, I want the job.
And let me keep just one foot in the pigshit too
this much straddle I can do

and I'll harpoon a whale from a pram for you
my hairy chest blown like the poet's beard.
I wonder if he'll offer me a job,
anything to clear the air. I want my car. Sweaty palms
then—cosmic belch—I'm on the road again
the sun still battling clouds for parcels of Madonna,
my car restored at least another hundred miles
I pay the 27.60 relieved,
boy on bicycle sees me coming,
crosses road, dismounts,
then pulls bike up over curb & waits
till car and I have gone
and I'm home, glad to be home,
glad for that part of a life that can go
into words, glad to see how silly you are, harpoon man

and me and 27.60 shot & damn
now it's up to the *knees*
in piggy feces, how was I to know
(a mere 12 hours ago)
I was gonna hitch half the whole way?

COMET COME

If I could make clear
Come Heaven streaking blue light stronger than sun's
If I could wipe the stains off retina
& iris & we could gaze & gaze
Into each other's silent vision.

Clouds hang on mountain tops here for days
They seal us out. Yet the hardest knowledge
Came one cloudless night
I saw a shooting star
& tried to show it to my friend.

How difficult to share perceptions
While they are still intact!
Is it divine protection (perfection?)
That delays the shutter,
Keeps the deer in front of the bullet?

I want to test the atmospheric freeway
You burn through, want to know
Can you warm us in time
& close the holes behind you.
Will you draw the oceans up & over us as prophesied in Luke?
If I could only share your unlikely flowering
Instead of riding this downward slump
Like a country out of oil, jerking still.
Like a casket lowering,
You march your mystery through my mind

Light years compacted in the briefest flash.
You make me want to throw up
My hands in delight, ask man
To perform the incredible
Like hold fire.

DABBLING IN OILS

words failing
I paint you a face like a kneecap
a scoop of heaven soft & firm support
it turns desire to energy
then back again.

To know you once more in that impossible house
only by painting I can ever see:
such patience it takes, such a drive's required
greater than dredging up words
to know foreground vs. background,
what should be the big thing in front
to give the rest perspective,
and where's the vanishing point Miss Cheek

tried to teach me about when I was in school,
too young to care?

Mixing colors slows me down
I back off & raise a thumb.
& not because I know what to do
I sight along the thumb, exhale
& move back in, it's time to sign

ink spilling from your doorway,
the shadow of an emptied house.

VISION

Excited by the mountain range
I point it out to Ben.

"Oh yeah," he says, returning to his book.
How quickly children absorb beauty!

THE MOON

lasted all night & seemed to burn
toward noon
after just that brief blue darkness
nightfall bound by worlds.

And we turn to that rising
again & again
we turn and like stars, like debutantes,
like false teeth
we come out.

How would we know
blinded by words
as we are

the blood guess of morning on the rocks
how it dawns on the gulls
creak of their throats against salt wind.

NATURE POEM

Weather's its own cliché. The beauty
of ice crystals like diamonds or stars:
we are coal, we form under pressure
into greatest worth or else we're best
reduced under fire to the smudge.

Darkness covers these hundreds of small towns
like Carbondale, N.Y., where Rob and I
damn near drove off the sheer cliff
in fog our lights at midnight worth less
than the NoDoz. I had told him, "each time

I drive through Carbondale all I get's static
on the radio" and, "This, I know,
is where I am going to die." Just that
suspicion plus the bumpy progression
of ourselves and vehicle down unknown

foggy ways caused me to stop, get out,
investigate on foot the road—or whatever
it was we were traveling.
I get thankful for such chances of wisdom
and sulky they aren't sustained flashes

of brilliance useful for more than just saving the skin.
Now snow has claimed all the outdoor toys,
even my car's too far under to get me
anywhere, batteries on radio useless
to hear beyond the local drift;

Stay clear of Carbondale, dig pressure,

and those little molecules, the children,

spin off in song.

THE LAST WORDS

Oh Heavens! Such a
tiny airplane & the pilot's
a wacky straight who got his training free
during Vietnam.

Something unfortunate occurs with an aileron
I don't understand but it means curtains
and all we can do is fly around as low as possible
until the gas runs out.

The winds toss us considerably and the radio says
we're too far off course, of course, to pinpoint, we'll have
to chance it, crash land in the darkness on the mountainside
when the final spiral

down begins.
There. It is fairly clear we are going to die.
I turn to the pilot
and tell him how wonderful he's been

how he's been the most important bullshit
in my life I am not thinking to speak of you

oh God

DECEMBER 8, 1980

—in memory of John Lennon

Ice on the trees like diamonds
breaks them, some of them,
usually the weakest
but now and then one
that, reaching maturity, is just at the stage
when all sorts of shapes are possible.

When the causes of those shapes,
like storms or overgrowth of other trees that fall,
are so quickly gone, so ill perceived and unremembered,
the surviving tree bears witness:
beauty grows from adversity
and is sustained by luck.

Knowing the chancy nature of things we look for meaning,
when the expression or utterance
of their being is all we can humanly do,
or groan or yell or make a song
whose voice is one person
brought down and hushed in the snow.

CONFESSION

One night a dense fog covered our meadow
and all the valley. I was searching
for a ewe, separated from the flock
and bleating, moving in what we'd perceive
in clear daylight as a romp.
She was panicked and finding her
in that thick darkness
was like trailing a cricket. I've never known

whether that movable chirp is one cricket scampering
or a whole confederacy
bent on decoying the search to oblivion.
What came in the sky dispelling fog and darkness
in an instant precipitated a quick, drenching shower.
It radiated enormous heat
but had blowers that dispersed it,
all with an eery whir. It was as if the sun had moved
closer to the earth, and thus had burned through
the night fog. The whirring stopped,
a fluorescent glare dimmed
and this enormous aluminum (?) gridded disk, no
bigger than a flat-roofed city school,
dropped fifty feet, claimed by gravity, and
settled as if it had merely rolled off
pavement onto gravel.

I could hear the ewe, frantic,
searching for a warm nuzzle or a pull of milk,
the arrival of this craft no more unsettling
than her immediate problem.
For me, the priorities got reversed.
I was tingled and chilled
from the sunburn effect of its arrival.
Though frightened, I could not bolt
to the uncertain safety of my house.
Curiosity, awe, and some queer notion
of responsibility held me there, clearing my throat
and touching my hot face
like someone who's just knocked on the door
for an important interview.

Almost in seconds, time seems distorted,
a giant tongue of foam poured out
and from it stepped two well-lit
beings, not unlike us in shape,
and capable of similar movement,
without special suits or space gear,
having heads that sported no faces
but blank polished steel (?) with grids,
miniatures of the space craft's belly!

The foam tongue withdrew
as they stood inches from me,
making no sound, giving off a pleasant glow.

The foam tongue was out again in moments
and they fell back into it and were
drawn into the ship, which
departed with neither noise nor heat, as if lifted.
The fog closed back in
and the ewe had backed into a fence corner
where I rescued her. In the morning
my face was so sore I couldn't shave
but there were no signs on the meadow,
not even a trace of foam, not the slightest
indentation where the thing had landed.
I have an uncle who once experienced something similar:
he told the story freely to reporters
until he saw that people laughed at him.

A quiet man whose vision on his meadow
was the meat for what he saw as public scorn,
he became obsessed with proving he had not lied
and was quickly detained and made a ward
of the state, where, bug-eyed with the constant effort to convince
his fellow patients that he saw a flying saucer,
he to this day resides.
Of course I won't go telling him,
that would only fuel his ardor,
but I'll learn from his lesson
how we do have responsibility, compulsion
to report:
my duty herein dispatched, this account.

THE FLIES

The flies are wakened by February thaw
and the first good hot stoked fire
since New Year's
when I never really got the cabin warm.

The flies are still groggy
as I help them out the window
and wave goodbye with a book of poems
I've used to scoop them from the sill.

God had a purpose for every animal
I remind myself
and in the dead of winter
and all else fails, think of flies:

their purpose is to make you glad
it's not summer.

BLUEBIRD

The way that male bluebird hammers to soup
a bug against the top of a phone pole!
He flies it down to his children
in the special box, a bluebirdhouse,
first landing on the roof and, inside,
the cheeping starts, they hear his feet upstairs
and begin complaining: I'm the hungriest,
I'm the hungriest. He faces the choice his mate
was forced to make a minute earlier.
When he leaves the house his bill contains their scat,
reminding me of the armless, single mother on TV
who kept her infant out of the state's clutches
by showing how she kept it clean,
a human accomplishing with her tongue
what almost every other species takes for granted.

Each year I let my family go
to Iowa, I drive them to the airport or station
and put them in the hands of a system,
then cultivating plants enjoy the habits of birds
that pass unnoticed or avoid
our land when children are calling.
The bluebird teaches me a dedicated humility.
He has no poems to write in precious solitude
against the fading, perfect afternoon.

He's got bugs to hammer and shit to take
from that black hole filled with squabbling.
Yet he sings upon the telephone wire
and makes the bluest blur as he hovers mid-air
to take another hapless bug on the wing!

And lo he never cultivates the corn
as I swat flies and sweat in the stupid garden
and look at what I've built
against the telephone pole,
crudely hammered from prefab parts,
illegal use of public utility, his home
and that of his ungrateful, awkward chicks.

DEBATE

On the stack of cherry firewood
cut in a sweat last August
2 squirrels alternate and squabble
for dominion. The off-squirrel
soothes his feelings foraging
under the hanging feeder.

He urges the chickadees
to nudge the feeder, chucks at them
to spill their seed
while the lordly squirrel preens at the top
of my wood, and with piggish eye
regards his peer.

Tails up, they also engage
in races over the crusted snow
in and out of brush piles and up the giant dead pine
for a stand-off on the second lowest limb.

Last spring 2 downy male woodpeckers
in a mating altercation
tumbled repeatedly to the ground
until I pounced on them and captured one.

He blinked, repentant,
as I cupped and admonished him

in the ways of peace,
then released him to the sky where
without missing a beat his wings unfolded
and carried him back to the fight.

RECIPE

What will you feed your future dinner?
Liquid seaweed.
                            You'll feed it liquid seaweed.
This is 99 cents for four liquid ounces, so make it go far
by watering down at a ratio of 1:600.
(Make sure the *1* part is the liquid seaweed.)

Now you got yourself a thriving plant,
what you going to do with it?
Out on the windowsill but bring in at dusk
or whenever the nights threaten to go below freezing.
(Here that means you need a lot of indoor space,
especially if you're bringing the peas and potatoes in each night.)
When danger of frost is past, set plant out in garden,
pluck away weeds and try not to water. Let the roots grow deep
in search of greater moisture and warmth
than fickle human caring, the occasional hose
or the equally fickle uncaring of the heavens can provide:
let it be, but keep the weeds away.

What will you feed your future dinner?
Give it green cow manure or whatever you can find
that helps add bulk to the earth,
not just little pellets from the factories.
Your soil needs *stuff,* not quick jolts
of speed that rob it of vitality.

Take tomato plants that have fought and gone leggy
for the little light that makes it through your window,

and lay roots and stem horizontal in a trench,
two inches deep, cover with potting soil and heap good green cow dung
on top to make a mound.
                              Do this in full sunshine then run for cover
you got tomatoes exploding from the earth
like the wildest dreams of Generals,
spaghetti sauce dripping from the clouds.
Bubbling earth, we treasure
your bounty, your visual possibility, the glory
of our cooking spread beyond political borders,
geographical zones erased, television flattening all terrain
great waves of radio and inhumanity
baking in the polar stew.

Excuse this digression. You gotta believe
there's gonna be a September to start reading this recipe anyway.
So you take the plant and keep its roots moist and warm
and feed it until it starts feeding you
or the raccoons:
a subject of great interest. Don't shoot
raccoons, don't try to fence them out.
Don't tie your biggest dog to the garden fence
because raccoons will kill it.
And don't try to wave them off once they know the corn's aripening.

Surround your corn with a field of cucumbers,
or failing that at least a band of them, four feet thick,
and space four paper cups filled with beer in the cucumber bed
and outside of that stake human hair
in those airy nets that once held onions,
and turn a transistor radio tuned to a wild all night disco station
in a plastic sack to protect it from rain
up full volume every night at sundown.
Raccoons won't want to dance to all that music,
and will assume the flat, tepid cups of beer
are all that remains of a bad party. Don't ask me
what role the human hair plays,
though I cannot recommend this scheme without it.

The pot is set to boiling before you go out for the harvest.
Likewise, before I go fishing, I chill my favorite chablis

and build the fire, for the fish
just jump
into my hands and I wrestle them, like my vegetables
back to the waiting fire,
stoked more by hunger, imagination, than by nuclear fuels or hardwood,
the fire that drives the germs away, the fire that tenderizes,
the fire for which this recipe's prepared.

FRESH CORN

That clever Mrs. Wright knows
how bad we want it fresh,
so when I peel the husk
and peek at rows of gol-
den flesh and ask "When was it picked?"
she slurs her Yankee drawl
just right and makes it sound
like "Just today" as she
replies "Why yesterday!"

TYPOGRAPHICAL ERRORS

Don't let them bother you, she said
After all, those are just worlds.

WRESTLING TO LOSE

None of us were winners, like
Armentrout or Beebe, the heavyweight
who surprised opponents twice his size
in the Unlimited Division, flipping one
who still scowled from the peevish handshake
that had to start each match.

Spring Weekend my parents drove my date up from New Jersey
and I wrestled the 135 pounder from Peddie

who took 30 seconds to pin me Spring Weekend
the year before. My father
clapped my back in the locker room
and pronounced it "a moral victory."

Behind the gym two weeks later
the hacks on the team smoked their first cigarettes
since fall and chafed at the gung hoes
who were still running laps. Where are they now?
Well, Armentrout's big in business for sure,
and Beebe's a famous neurosurgeon!

And us hackers? I'll hazard our wages
per capita can't touch *theirs.* We were artists,
idealists, the boys who invented wrestling to lose:
slam yourself down on the mat. With shoulders flat
hold your opponent just three seconds over you
helpless in the victory pose.

DOWN EAST

On the Maine coast, gains accomplished by the sea
reverse twice a day or after floods
over the years. Nature never learns
and neither does your so-called "man" ever learn,

ever learn a damn thing. She keeps herself busy
volcanoing it all to Kingdom Come
then smoothing over for ages while scratching
his chin, he calls for bigger studs.

NOT IN TIGHT LINES

Not in tight lines go the drops
of melting snow
each brightest
in the flash it glistens
from snow into water, then quickly too heavy

to be held, rolls off the snowbank's diminishing edge
joining not in tight lines
a muddy rivulet beneath which stones are polished
and worms wait it out, a little short of breath,
in the tight, dry subsoil.
In spring we all come out, not in tight lines
but surely less constrained

than the water, a river of people with rototillers
and fancy plans for improving the homesite.
There goes Mr. Delaney on his riding mower
and his wife Dolores, Dolores Delaney, pretty through the fat,
carrying the steel rake like a soldier on parade.
We are not in tight lines to march with the river
or to arrest its flow, not either little drops
brilliant at last and just for a moment
because, water and bone, each of us
contains a unique wish, a murmur,
flower louder
toward the ocean as a babble.

THE CHALLENGE

So what kind of poetry you write?
he finally asked after smoking in silence
half the cigarette he'd borrowed.
Waiting for my flowers and moons he thought up
the one he wrote about a dying white
horse in Vietnam, how the Montagnards
wouldn't let the Tennessee GIs put it out
of its misery and they were going crazy
seeing it—guts blown out—suffer.
This was what he brought home
and after hearing my credentials told me
that if he could write it, he would.
Was I serious enough? Did I care?
Would I just tack on a fourteenth line to make it a sonnet?

THE KIND OF POETRY I WRITE

I told him I think poetry is the language
that shares experience, not what is beautiful,
and I don't think I can use "moon" in my poems.
Of course, explaining it in a poem is kind of creepy.

I'm delighted someone would read this far,
and I never believed he'd listen:
each word a new chance
not to abuse an old cliché,

not to construct self-conscious language,
not to be beautiful, not to confound,
not to take a risk, not to discover, share,
not to be mystical,

that was what I was not writing for these days!
And I was sure depressed about it all.
I told him I'd published in a magazine.
"Resting on your laurels, eh?" he said.

Yeah, resting on my laurels
and driving home what I took to be the moon
—a smudge of light above Montpelier—
glowed like the top of a smokestack
and I kept driving along and my poem said
I never saw it I never said it.

VANTAGE

—for H.C.

My Mexican jumping beans
came in 2 small, square plastic boxes,
each large enough to hold a dozen
but containing just four so buyers would hear them click,
their beans bouncing
against the plastic, added walls
like the hearts of caged turtles.

The cashier could guarantee
each package to contain at least one bean
that would jump two months or more.

I took them to Chicago
where, in my hotel room, I cut the worst open,
thumbnailed a soft spot the others didn't have.
I planned to shake this bean empty
            that had never in my presence jumped.
And quickly alarmed on looking in I saw
the pallid pillar gazing back. Later recounting to my friend
(an alumnus of what he calls "the hatch"), I said
at first I was sorry to have wrecked a good bean,
then wondered why the pillar didn't come out.
"He was probably wondering why the hell *you* didn't come *in*."

We spent time in Iowa where I gave the
best beans away.
We stopped in Detroit, had a light snack on the airline in Cleveland, and
home in Vermont, the 3 beans remaining were still okay, though aging,
persistent warriors against the injustice of their being
(or continual celebrants, who knows why they dance?),
but losing their curiosity value
except at night. I'd hear them click
from deep inside the bag still packed with summer clothes,
then less until no more.

Farewell Bassie, goodbye Salimoney,
remember me to Olydia, brave beans.
Guaranteed two months you spanned a season,
and to my ultimate surprise, today,

my opened suitcase gave a click
and there the one I thought I'd killed
still bangs around somehow having sealed the cut
I made in his shell.

FATHERHOOD

I found a piece of used chewing gum on the table:
is this yours? I asked my son, holding the disgusting glob up
for him to see.
I don't know, toss it to me,
he replied with a shrug and a look of studied concern.

The kid's got a quick mind and he's gone seriously punk.
There's nothing I can do to keep up, or in any way
to match his irreverent perception of irrelevance.
What makes the Valley Doll giggle is the
unconnectedness of things, the little private leaps
the brain makes between the items on a
conversation's agenda, it is a private
irreverent creativity these rotten kids share,
and we attribute it to the fads that prevailed
in our own time, dope, whiskey, rock
music, or too much TV.

I can't keep up with it, nor will I try.
Instead I'll enjoy its absurdist tendencies
and hope my kid doesn't become so smart he
outwits himself and winds up with a handful of
soggy bubble gum. If I can remember how
much I had to teach my father, I can
allow my son that satisfaction.

FOR ANNA

Your father lectures you on canoe safety.
He says the slightest shift
can fill the boat with water, so be still.

And having sat you safely in the center
of its floor, lets himself in
talking all the time—now notice how I keep

weight low and to the center, he preaches
as the side goes under and he swamps it.

In these thin waters, a seasonal marsh
that comes to life each spring with peepers,
there is little danger of drowning as long as one
doesn't try to swim but stands
in the knee-deepest parts.
And he does and so do you, both sputtering.

After helping him beach and empty the canoe,
with the wisdom and trust of a child
you insist that he be first, then board his boat again!

THOSE STARS

You think those stars are telling us something,
They are. They're winking. Heaven's eyeballs,
Points of diamonds, the far edge of sunlight
Too distant to blind the normal eye.

When the wind is dead you'll hear
The sound of fingers crossing
Uncrossing, the fingers that define
And hold the limits of this universe

Like a large, transparent basketball.
Come on they flutter and throw it all up
So the stars jiggle and a few go out
Before we notice, but catching

And cupping it again those hands
Forget a second throw for maybe eons—
Long enough for faith to develop
On a few of the planets supporting life.

Now we want a way to get our friendly vibes
Known to the owner of those hands,
Who surely if s/he knew us here
Would set the whole thing down most carefully.

THE DAMP OCTOBER

leaves fell in clumps
and browned before their brighter colors

could hold

I remember well the mud tracks
dragged across the floor,
dried to heavy dust by noon & swept out the door
puffing I shall return

bum's rush
we always think we got our dirt by the scruff

how we treat the heart
how we use soil as a verb

MISSING THE PROOF

In my own little world
I rush against the passing season
and try to get a start on the season coming:
winter cut wood for next winter;
springtime get the tiller going
haul manure and fence the garden right this time;
summer pull weeds and build a chicken coop;
fall stack wood and cut wood that didn't get cut last winter.

The sun inches lower in the sky each day,
and starts back up before winter is even half started,
season after season, eventually so far behind
winter finds me cutting wood one day to burn the next until
I build a fire to warm me in the woods
and burn what I cut so there's nothing to haul home
and in panic my family searches my flushed face
demanding me to prove I worked all day.

My young daughter sniffs where her nose reaches my belly
and remarks I smell like cutting wood

while my older son and wife look me in the eye
for a trace of lost confidence.
They have huddled at the stove all day waiting.
Perhaps tomorrow they will be cold enough to help,
but for the night we sleep in the same bed
under heaps of blankets pooled from our rooms.

I dream of my own importance in life
until by some breach of common sense
I feel that I have been the constant
and the sun an incidental body on the run.

MOONLIGHT

The boss thinks
      I'm devoted to my family.
At home they say
      I'm married to my work.

SYLLABLES

Though every generation claims its share of Frosts,
the only real or self-appointed Frost was Robert Frost himself.
Anyway, you need a name for an accolade? Mantel of syllables
or letters embossed on special license plates,
Look out! That big white Lincoln whooshed
past your wagon on the interstate.
If you could have kept up you'd have tailgated,
trusting inside the reflective glass rode a radar detector,
you could speed with impunity. Or perhaps it was a sting:
ambitious cop from Washington
ready to arrest you or a state trooper
off duty, driving home at dusk in an official car,
accepts bribe in the twilight
and winds up in the slammer for a year.

Vermont's got its prisons but when a man from Florida,
visiting his second summer in a row,

learned we have six "correctional" facilities
for adult law-breakers, his mouth dropped.
He'd been upset the week before to hear
Frost wasn't born in Vermont, but this time
he nearly cried. I could have mentioned other institutions.
He wasn't so interested that inmates need contact
with the world's ideas and people as by the fact
that in St. Albans and St. Johnsbury, in Burlington
and Windsor, Rutland and Woodstock
are jails. I changed the subject and he relaxed
enough I got my point across
about the book we were discussing.

The prison with the nicest coordinator
had the loudest iron doors,
visitors constantly reminded
what inmates take for granted
as a fetus adjusts to its mother's breathing
or miners adapt to conditions that kill them.
David Budbill's poems were the subject.
The cultural coordinator said she often found
his book's Vermonters "stick figures—personality types."
A young inmate from Tennessee:
"If so it's because Vermonters
didn't let the author close enough to them."
These syllables from one with three more years
in a place some people don't know exists.

Another participant expressed contempt:
"That writer's got it made. Play was produced here in town."
But when the poems passed his expectations,
they touched him with familiar syllables,
arranged in another version of the truth: he liked the book.
The people of Vermont are not just the Yankee farmers,
whose "industry" crumbled in twenty years,
with 2,739 of 5,264 dairy farms gone since 1969.
The growth in tourism eased the sting
and like as not farmers
from the '70s tend ski lifts and bars
on gorgeous mountain tops or drive trucks

or work at the university or in state government
or sell hardware, teach school, edit, chair committees

while 2,500 still hay the fields and milk cows
for which Vermont is famous. As malls and shopping centers
replace the dairy herds and crops, what's a man to do?
Frost would have captured it with irony
and maybe played a hand in helping to reverse
a stone's fate in quicksand, nearly my fate once
when marching through a neighbor's barnyard to collect
on a debt, I got two feet
into the manure pit and sinking fast
finally figured to reverse direction.
My neighbor never said, when I asked for the check,
"We'd never have missed you," though he could tell
from the level of things in the air,
and on my trousers, where I'd been.

The people of Vermont? You'll know them
one or two at a time, not through annual Town Meetings
or around a single ritual like sugaring or potluck dinners,
and they'll fool you. You've got to be persistent,
a journalist, unless you've got a lifetime.
So when I asked Hugh Gross "How was sugaring this year?"
he said "Not bad." I rephrased the question, knowing it
had been a banner year. "Best season ever?"
"Yup."
          You'll know them one or two at a time,
and they'll fool you. When I arrived in '68,
I admired a house painter whose Yankee savvy
and accent obscured that he had lived
all but the past six years in New Jersey,
my home too. The cussedest Yankees

are the ones who got here late and have
to make up time like the Happy Trails Lady
never smiling except in the woods
or the woman from Scotland who won't look humans in the eye
unless she's about to let them take a pet
from her pound. She hates people for the abuse
she sees animals suffer.

                    The next cussedest Yankees
are the Yankees themselves: take Harold, the farmer
whose old house and fields I bought when he quit farming
at sixty-five to drive the town tractor, maintain town roads,
grading and cutting brush. One summer day I was barefoot,
shirtless in shorts when he stopped to visit, yelling down
over the hot diesel engine, his blade
in thick roadside grass inches short

of a large rock. When we'd done talking
I sweated that rock, as he watched, from his path: I squatted
and worked it up, over and behind the cutter bar.
He smiled, touched his cap, lurched into gear and drove
up the road.
        The backstrap of his cap
winked in the bright afternoon as I saw the cutter bar raise
from its grass-height position
over some new roadside obstacle.

I built a chimney for the oil furnace I'd installed to replace Harold's
kerosene space heater. I never was told to mix sand with the mortar, so
the chimney blocks, hefted up a ladder leaned to the side of the third
story and braced by an ancient house, were never really leveled. The
final result had shape in common with a tall letter "S." Wendell Savage,
who grew up in the house before Harold bought it, saw the chimney,
smiled and scratched his chin, "I never saw smoke that wouldn't bend."
This phrase ever since has lessened my shame at not reading details
in the how-to books.

This morning I woke to thoughts of Patricia
and what's happened to her mother?
who used to walk her forty year old Patricia
through Montpelier and take her to the fairs
and big art openings, always in a matching yellow outfit,
Patricia equally bright in red or shocking pink.
When I was really awake I tended my face and dressed,
then saw Patricia on my way to work!
Her mother has probably died. "Dead as a flapped jack"
Patricia uttered in my morning dream,
the nearly waked state where a distant figure

becomes friend for life, someone you see
and care about, on the street
in color if I dream in color,
the syllable or building block of lasting vision.

No death will keep Patricia at her mother's heel.
She walks Elm Street and goes in muted colors
to the fairs with a bigger smile
than ever. We're both out on the streets
and glad to live where we're needed.
Where notice of the mountains seems important,
where, after frost, leaves brown and scramble from the trees—
each a syllable in a long, hard sentence:
Winter—things become clear.
                              On a good November day I can see
six miles when even yesterday the view for the leaves was just ten feet.
The seasons keep me going, keep me hoping I can count
or somehow keep up with my debt,
my interest on my debt,
to Patricia and all others with whom on this planet I move.

THE SANDMAN

So I was coming around the corner and the car ahead of me has stopped
and I'm on sheer ice and my car starts to skid and there's this guy on
the sidewalk with a shovel and just before my car crunches into the
car ahead of me he throws a shovelful of sand under my rear tires and
my car comes to a stop ten feet from disaster.

Half an hour later I'm at the Xerox machine with a job I've gotta have
copied in time for the mail, which leaves in ten minutes and the machine
jams and I'm trying to get the paper out and something throws a spark
and ignites the paper so smoke is starting to curl from the ink drum and
I'm trying to figure whether I should run to the men's room for a handful
of water when this guy appears with a shovel and throws a shovelful of
sand into the machine's underbelly and the smoking stops.

FOR HAYDEN

The tourist, happy to be alive in a place like Vermont,
turns to the local stuck here twelve months a year
and says "Where do *you* go to get away?"
Then corrects himself with a quick addition:
"Of course anyone lucky enough to *live* here
            doesn't need to get away!"
And that's the end of friendship there,
the loss of universal feeling
to a lie, in this case a patronizing one
because the local knows
that s.o.b. can choose
and he's here only three days a year!

The tourist moves closer to the barbwire fence
for a better view of the farmer
astride his tractor with the side-bar cutter
and the grass is falling in waves parallel
to the last row that was felled
while the squared-off stand remaining
gets surrounded smaller and smaller.
The cutter doesn't jam and the tourist
thinks that's the farmer's life and I shared it
for ten minutes while he squared
his field and made hay.
Meanwhile, farmer thinking:
that poor bastard got some time off from the city
and best he can do is watch me drive.
Thank God nothing's going wrong.

And fingers a dincher from the floor of his pack
as the tourist turns
back to the waiting family and automobile,
a family that never chose to cease
bickering and exit the car, but instead to sweat
and call periodically for him to drive them on.
The farmer on his tractor cannot watch them at all times
cornering the field, he cannot look back
            as they disappear, his vision
is the stop-frame picture of their positions

every time his tractor is headed straight down the row
toward their parking spot,
each time the father, now grown familiar with his foot on a strand,
gazes at him in the foreground, the carful of family
parked in the shade, exasperated,
behind. He makes another square,
a little farther from them as he hays
toward dead center of the field.
When the tractor straightens to the row
that lets him see the tourists
they are gone.

They were too far off to see the field sparrow's well-hidden eggs
crumble under the cutter bar, and they would never recognize
the all-day, redundant, useless scold
of the field sparrow and her mate whose nesting grounds
and potential family have been unbelievably erased
        lined up in horizontal rows
        like grease stains on an earthen plate.

They left too soon to hear the cutter bar clank
against another grass-hidden object
        this time not eggs, but stone,
and the ripping free of iron and the
        engine's overheated coughing to a stop
in gritty, diesel-wafting heat.
The scold is darting at the farmer as he tries to
coax the wounded cutter back on the bar.
Only a square of grass remains to be mowed
and the tractor's engine is rough to restart in this heat.
He gooses and coughs it back into action,
jumps free and checks the motion of the bar.
It works and back he climbs, too high
to see the minute dangers of his work,
too far from the retreating tourist
rehearsing for Monday's coffee break
as he describes to wife and children
what they sat through and never saw
anything there to start with.

EDGE

The tooth that I broke
using it instead of a knife
now has an edge
more useful than a knife.

THIS IS GROSS

but I cough up a good one
and whistle-thrust it through my lips
into the blazing furnace fire
where it catches halfway up a maple chunk
and sleazes into a giant teardrop
before starting to sizzle.

This is gross but it begins to puff up,
having sealed and trapped sufficient air
to expand it to the size and shape
of a giant cocoon: it seems to pop
but returns from half inflated to its greatest girth
repeatedly, breathing like a heart confused.

At last I understand how fire might make the parts of life
and, from the popping seed they issue, rudiments of speech.

THE WATER

The water was doing what water does best,
which is soak things.
Which is finding its own level.
Which is leading to growth—plant growth
and then rot which is back to the thirsty soil.

The water was doing what water does best,
it was dripping from every surface,
it was dripping from my hair and from my nose,

fingertips and elbows and from the cuffs of soaked pants
through socks into shoes.

And the nasty November wind was doing what it does best
which is to take thin blood and flesh
to the just short of numb stage, Christ the water,
without that wind, would have seemed almost *warm*.
I was cursing my luck, out of gas, two miles from home

on a deserted country road, I was walking!
At 6 p.m. I was leaning into the driven rain,
not seeing any humor through wet lashes,
but already savoring the telling later,
around the fire, attentive audience, cocoa steaming in clay mugs:

the wind was whipping bullets of water
against my helpless face, while river currents
forced me backwards nearly half the time.
But I sang in the gathering darkness,
sang and brought my soggy groceries home,

doing what I do best.

ORSON

The neighborhood beagle, ignored by family,
hated by the neighbors, is a car runner,
garbage eater, chicken killer who is,
nevertheless, kind with children
and has always treated me with decency
even if he does chase my car.
Shot and wounded, rumor had him dead
but we saw him the next day,
about the time Reagan was shot.
The owners kept him on a chain for a while,
but by the time Reagan was back in the Oval Office,
Orson was back on the loose, raising hell
and none the wiser for his brush with death.

Today, a first real spring-like Sunday,
he sauntered down our lane. I called him
to make friends, then as he came and got petted
I wondered would he misunderstand my attentions
and return for my chickens,
my car, my trash?

PIGSKIN

Spiro with a long i
is our word for spiral,
something I could never throw
except by luck
until this year.

With small hands
as a boy I couldn't hold
the fat pigskin
and carried into adulthood
the habit of clutching fingers

that finally found a hold
with the introduction of the pennyweight
rubbery foam Nerf ball
to a game that had formerly
left me frustrated.

Proud that my fingers could grasp
defiance of gravity,
I held the Nerf for every throw
so hard that my son Ben, on catching it,
would claim I'd left imprints

in the foam. "Cratered like the moon"
he'd crow, returning my heave
with an effortless spiro, the ball
all smoothed by the time
it spun into my arms.

By some mistake I got smart
a couple weeks ago and threw
before my fingers clamped
and the ball went out
to everyone's amazement like a bullet.

Within a day or two
I'd discovered and practiced my mistake
and now my son and I toss perfect spiros
back and forth until my arm gives out
and the ball is bored without bruising

and wobbling through the sky, bouncing wide,
bobbling off the edge of the hill,
chased by Ben who screams:
"Stop! Come back! Bad throw!"

INTRODUCTION

Let me introduce to you the theory
of backwards evolution.
But first an aside:
words backwards tell a lot about themselves,
Radar backwards is radar, a one-word palindrome.
Backwards backwards is sdrawkcab,
and—get this—embargo backwards is o grab me,
catatonic is cannot attack, dermatitis, sit tight I'm red,
constitute, two tits knock, and revolution is no shoe lover.
I can say whole sentences backwards
without prior consideration, accurate
unless you work one up ahead of time
to trick me. Language loved and played with
like a child reveals itself.

Backwards evolution, by the bye,
holds simply that our entire perception
of cause and effect is merely reversed:
think about it.

Effect and cause. Effect *then* cause.
Meanwhile our memories are upside down
because provably at birth we reach up
when we should reach down, meaning
our vision "has to be trained."
And so I have no prophetic "vision"
but say it all starts in the future as we see it
with a big bang,
the sun-like energy, the god that sets us spinning
and we evolve to this day,
each of us growing younger
feeling it's the other way around.

Let me introduce you to
this born again theory
which leads us all backwards to our birth and
takes the world unmistakably backwards before that
to the big bang creation where, I believe, it all
starts spinning the other way again, playing out
toward the day when you got born, then me
or the other way around
depending on which way the world is spinning,
which bounce of the big bang we're on.
Free choice? Forget it.
You've worn notches in the grooves of bang-prescribed
         human activity. You are going to scratch
         your left temple tonight at bedtime
         just as you will next bang around,
         except on that trip through you
         will first scratch and only then feel the itch.
         Old 16 mm movies played backwards,
         the diver emerging feet first from the center of the pool,
         through the air until she balances on the board,
         then backs confidently away, all dry.
         Except on film we never see it that way
         because of seeing upside down at birth.
         Oh, never mind, you're too stupid anyway.

But can't you just see the sense of things flying back together,
the compost recomposing into real banana peels,

the banana reentering your body to put it politely as I can
and being undigested, unchewed, and emerging
from your mouth only to have the peel replaced,
the whole thing driven backwards to the supermarket
from where it is eventually untugged to Costa Rica
and hung back on the tree,
which resorbs it as it goes from green
to whatever they are before then?

Meanwhile, presidents and kings are unwaging wars
and back away from their jobs
which fall into the laps of those who are ready to retire.

THE SAILOR

In my movie the boat goes under
And he alone survives the night in the cold ocean,
Swimming he hopes in a shoreward direction.
Daylight and he's still afloat, pawing the water
And doesn't yet know he's only fifty feet from shore.
He goes under for what will be the last time
But only a few feet down scrapes bottom.
He's suddenly a changed man and half hops, half swims
The remaining distance, hauls himself waterlogged
Partway up the beach before collapsing into sleep.
As he dreams the tide comes in
And rolls him back to sea.

MOTH

After you cut the lights tonight
all the moths will burst into tears
that haven't already singed their wings
on what they think is the marvelous sun,

those unconsolable little light worshippers
will beat their wings to powder night after night
until all that's left are miniscule coat hangers
like skeletons poking from their puffy moth bodies.
How does a moth know to love the light
or is it hatred, this unflagging devotion, an ill-concealed fury
that makes it dive toward the brightest
or the only lit bulb in the house?

So how does an all-white, all-male jury react
when you fall in love with a moth? This pet
you've cultivated, trained and seek to wed?
Will they show compassion and sanction the union

or separate you forever by pulling the plug on your freedom,
committing you for decades to a darkened, padded cell?
Or do you play it cool and encourage the moth to keep quiet,
be discrete, don't brag about your human lover?

Hide the candles! Whisk away all matches.
Fall in love with a moth and you got another moth to feed.

THE WIFE AGREES

The wife agrees to cut my hair.
She's the cheapest game in town
And it doesn't hurt too much
Except when she clips my ears.
I guess she doesn't like being called the wife.

The little woman says I'm getting cocky
And tells me from now on I need an appointment.
None of this springing it on her at the last moment
Before a poetry reading
Or the gathering of important committees,

Tugs at the forelock and shoves my head to the side,
Maintains that the shears are too dull,
And leaves a moth hole on the left side
About which I generously complain.
I guess she doesn't like being called the little woman.

But I'm not gonna stop my bitching
About looking like a half-peeled onion.
So she takes the scissors and chops a grocery bag in half.
"Put this on the left side of your head," she says.
"Then people can only see your better half."

HITCHHIKING FOR A HAIRCUT INTO HARRISBURG, PA

My hair is still long.

THE RIGHT WORDS

—for Jim

When I was a kid
and something bad happened to a neighbor
I tried to stay away until things had blown over:
I didn't know what to say.

My grandfather cut his left thumb clean off
with a table saw. He was a carpenter
making someone a table. He drove himself
to the hospital twelve miles

holding his red hand out the window at red lights
so traffic would know to let him through.
I didn't want to see him, no matter
that I loved him, hell, that made it harder,

but he was in our driveway before I knew
he was even out of the hospital
and before I could hug him or hide
he told me his thumb-stump had grown a new nail.

"Wanna see?" Tongue frozen
I nodded and saw
he held to his turbaned thumb
a six-penny nail from his shop.

A friend at a fancy dinner
asked her three-year-old son
who had just, by accident, farted loudly,
"Johnny, what do you say?"

The guests had paused in their talk
to study their reflections in the consommé.
The astonished child replied:
"Thank you."

What *does* one say, what *are* the right words?
My friend just lost half his house to a fire.

I said: "You're so calm.
I'd be throwing a fit."

He replied in a way that comforted me:
"I've thrown it already."

POTTER

Your hands at the wheel
pull a fat lump of clay,
almost will it,
up to a vase.

You make the hole with your thumb
and guide the flaring rim
so it stays round
but gets thinner and thinner

against firm fingers
now within the hole,
now a cavity,
your thumb started.

Your gray hand dips new water
to keep it pliable
and the rim takes an even finer tune
but you spot an imperfection,

with wire cut the spinning vase
down to a mixing bowl.

Another perfection check
reveals a new flaw
and the wire
reduces the clay to a cereal bowl.

Even that won't work
and the whole remaining lump bites the dust.
Recycled. I'm astonished
how quickly destroyed, something so fine.

LEAF PEEPERS

New Mercedes van
with Jersey plates,
stuffed with tourists
scowling at a conifer:

"Damn.
We got here too early!"

LIGHTNING TURKEY

—for Andy

I am a lightning turkey,
so named because I run and run,
run so fast the bullet can't catch up,
run so fast the grass beneath my feet catches fire.
I am a lightning turkey
the color of the wind and built for speed.
Built for speed so Thanksgiving doesn't faze me,
built for speed because I am always the day after Christmas,
built for speed for I am the whizzing wonder of the whole green earth
built for speed because my drums are for beating,
not eating, not cooking, not plucking, not stuffing,
not saying a prayer over and calling it grace
not washing me down with champagne
not picking me apart the days after the holidays.
Nor slicing me into sandwiches with lots of mayonnaise.
For I am a lightning turkey. My song will waken the world,
my scream will boil the blood of pilgrims,
my life will be an example.
For I shall be the president of all turkeys,
and from their bones, reconstruct the flesh
and put the guts back in from before they were dressed
and stick each feather back into its feather hole,
replace the heads and beaks, the tongues and wattles,
and set them fluttering back in life's barnyard,
endowed with my speed, my appetite for man.

UPSIDE DOWN

Upside down, my pants hang from the line
Depending from a pair of wooden clothespins
One to each leg. The waist is three inches too high
To scuff the leaves, though six weeks from now
We'll have to raise the line or double
The trousers over at the thighs to keep the waist
From dragging snow. Come a good January thaw
We could hang a pair by the cuffs and let the waist freeze
Into the puddle where melted snow froze fast
At the snap end to the thaw, then
Unpin the cuffs and remove the line so a flat pair of pants
Is stiff and vertical upside down executive
Who plunged head first into the earth, up to his waist!

THE VIEWMASTER

I keep trying to lock you in
get my eyes to cross just so
the right image
merges with the left image
and the brain picks up a 3-D message.

To escape in lost focus!
As if looking at a picture long enough
will allow me to wander in,
look around, see the back side of things,
an ordinary schmuck made important with a stage pass
intent on befriending the star

and kind of hoping the world will notice.

It's like the many small hexagonal tiles
on bathroom floors in old hotels,
I love to watch my bare feet disappear
into the ages as, The Thinker, fist bracing chin,
elbow on knee, I study the universe
into which my toes can wiggle, pad around.

But—no!—you have to bend
or otherwise distort my vision,
close me out when I think I've locked you in,
an amateur with love songs to an image on the page,
who would have you know him, not just vice versa,
a picture responding to its viewer.
An art we haven't yet explored.

DELICATE

It's delicate when we touch
each other, a careful mistake
will do but nothing more.
It's delicate the love
we carry and know
that only what waits
is separation
and let the new people
into your lives—
or is this just a bunch
of hopeful crap?

It's delicate too this learning.
How even with degrees no one said
there'd be a *job*, but there is work
o there is work. How many
times I vacuum each week
is a measure of unemployment
though vacuuming is nothing I do for enjoyment.

I want me one of them *riding* vacuums,
metallic green with special bumpers
so I don't mar the furniture as I'm whizzing the room,
caroming off the pillars of our old upright piano
and making the long run down the hall,
wearing the safety helmet that came with the unit,
          wielding the magic wand
attachment at cobwebs as I glide by.

Cobwebs! Don't make me think of them.
Let me picture a spider's more symmetrical effort,
not the chaotic gathering of dust
in strands that hang from ceilings.
Let me think of spider webs,
the organization of desire,
a spider's fractal-like construction to ward off starvation,
a sticky, silver trampoline with "plenty of space to fly through,
just avoid the center!" claims the stupid moth
that fouls the whole web and isn't
anything the spider wants,
just a dusty pair of wings, fluttered to a mealy core,
the cobweb of the animal world.

Not to speak of the damaged web to rebuild
for, though resilient, a spider web is delicate
and delicate is like touch, like love, like learning,
like the finest, most expensive, tiniest chocolate
you're only supposed to have one of.

THE ULTIMATE COMMUTE

Every day, same time, he sees her car
on the two lane highway, approaching his car
as they drive to their jobs in opposite directions.
He memorizes her license plate,
he falls in love
with that sensuous face in the windshield
and those two, tenuous hands on the wheel,
always in the proper ten-and-two-o'clock position,
glimpsed each day
as they whistle past each other
to their work in opposite directions.

How can he meet her?
He lacks the courage to call her license number in
to Motor Vehicles and ask for her name,
address, home phone and marital status
or some details on the color of her eyes,
at forty miles per hour plus forty miles per hour

in the opposite direction, that's eighty miles per hour
at ten feet the closest they've ever been,
it's a miracle he even knows she's pretty,
or is he imagining that, too?
And willing?

So the complications are daunting.
The only reason he doesn't leave his job
is he'd miss this Mondays through Friday most weeks,
daily, instantaneous rendezvous,
no more than five seconds
from spotting her grill to seeing the tail lights
in the rearview mirror,
he's started to dread the weekends
because he knows she loves these meetings too.
Wasn't that a weak smile she managed
and a tentative wave of the fingertips,

a moment of danger when one hand
nearly left the wheel in a hot flash,
tempestuous, impetuous, and
for that moment vulnerable I'm sure?
The whole expression was Be My Friend
but in her embarrassment she missed
his reciprocation the next day and the next:
he carried a yellow rose by the stem
between his teeth, thorns sometimes spiking
the roof of his mouth and one day at work
he nursed a pierced lip.

He knows that on the hottest days of all,
when his trousers are thin and the top is down,
she's probably wearing a short skirt
and rubs herself as he does, suggestively,
each out of sight of the other, maybe
just a sentimental and funny reminder,
maybe in lust lost on the highway
each day where it begins,
that little pep talk you can give yourself
and with all your aging confidence you know
she's giving herself too.

JUST KIDDING, HONEST

Your young son's young friend,
the one whose successful brain surgery
removed not all speech but, strangely,
his nouns: it turns out they'd also been stored
on the other side of his brain,
he just had to find them
and the access key was music,
all the TV and radio jingles starting with
Chicquita Banana and I'm Here to Say:
makes me more aware than ever
it's a fucking computer we carry
between our ears, these audio terminals,
and when I saw the special
on brain surgery I learned they pin little numbers
to the lobes where certain impulses register. Honest.

I guess everyone's wired a little different
so a naked nurse passes through intensive care
your hard-on tells 'em you noticed
and a 26 is pinned to the point in your brain
where the pulsing soon makes wisps of smoke
that sting the surgeons' eyes behind their masks
and the one with the good bedside manner makes a crack
how he now knows where to cut
if you ever wave that big dong at his wife. Just kidding.

It's a crude part of mine they'd want to pin down
and eliminate, cynical distrust and a laugh
that echoes from hemisphere to hemisphere,
here I am! here I am!
as, desperate for a target, in a pulse,
just kidding, honest, for a laugh,
the red-eyed, red-faced surgeons swipe their scalpels
or probe nouns and music with a swab
to rescue language, hoping for the truth.

  —for Ellen

TWO STORIES ON MY NAME

In high school I was Gee-off or Goof, never Geof. It was a hell of a deal having a name so often misused but I got used to it and when in college my writing teacher told me to publish under George or G.F., I knew that I was Geof forever. One night, on my way to a bookstore poetry reading featuring me, I saw the young woman I had previously seen only when she was walking. This time she was driving. She is obviously someone I had come to regard as an "extraordinary person" with the same objectivity employed when I buy a copy of *Playboy*, convincing myself I'm doing it for the interview. I saw her buy a copy of *The New Yorker* once at the newstand/convenience shop next to the bookstore. So I could excuse my lust for her to the fact she had literary interests! and now I see that the license plate on the car she's trying to find a parking space for is exactly the letters of my name. One fucking f, I can't believe it. Suddenly it hits me she's a silent admirer on her way to my reading and indeed she parks in the only remaining space in front of the bookstore. I find a spot to dump my car—I'm already five minutes late—and, taking care not to slip on the ice, bustle to the bookstore, manuscripts under my arm and hoping she was so late she had to take a front-row seat. I enter the bookstore just at the moment she is leaving the convenience shop next door, a pound of bacon shielding her purse from the rain. She is back in her car and revving the engine as I greet my small audience.

I got my name one night when my father, pissing his name in the snow, got Geo of George completed before he ran out of steam and simply added the F of his middle name as a dribbling flourish. (He later admitted he had been possessed of the arrogance to have intended pissing his whole name, including Frederick and the abbreviation for Junior.) Admiring his yellow shorthand in the snow, he saw a new way to spell Geof and rescued triumph from apparent defeat.

MOVING THE WOODPILE

Moving the woodpile I do my serious thinking:
Should I forswear speech, is my ego finally shrinking?
Questions posed against the health of sane activity,
The woodpile was there and should be here

And moved twice again before burning.
No matter where I place reserves
It's always wrong once the fire starts:
Too close for safety, too close for mere

Aesthetics, not pretty not functional, inconvenient,
Pure dangerous. So many excuses
To go electric! A nuke two hundred miles away
Might not burn us out the way this woodblaze

Wants free of its cast iron cell
Across the kindling, scattered dust
Across the cement floor to the bigger pile
And then to walls and joists and finally the roof.

A college kid at the ski slopes told me
Of his mother's home: she hopes it burns.
Because, he said, the timbers have rotted to kindling.
If it's taken by heat before wind moves it on,

Insurance will pay for their dream house,
No fairer price nor place on earth.

SIX HAIKU

The marionette
Works the scissors with both hands
Up to cut the strings

Wide V swims the sky
Each goose honks its own idea
Where to spend the night

Nasty Brussels sprout!
Best get off my plate. Ugly
Things get eaten too

Ancient icicle
You've been so hard all winter
Now sun brings your tears.

Tilting my head back
To take a drink, wow: 2 moons!
That's one too many.

Between Hemingway
And Homer you'll find my works
At better bookstores

PATH POEM

They say the daughter at birth has all the eggs
she'll ever produce: the path is set at your mother's birth
as other paths unfold like a lifeline
in the gradual, almost imperceptible unclenching fist of time.

Some of these paths will come to coincidence:
it might be the accident
of a flat tire that delays you just enough
to miss the train that would have run you over,

and driving home with your suitcase stop at a bar
to inspect the tire then decide to have one
and meet a brilliant executive
who takes you into her confidence and within the year

you're flying in a private jet, riding limousines
with faultless tires and tuxedoed drivers
who know the quickest route and where to drop you
to celebrate time saved by such smart travel.

At times you think *you're* controlling the path,
how else would anyone be so lucky
if they weren't just plain smart:
maybe a brilliant executive?

But you crave time so *you* can climb into the tuxedo
and take *yourself* for a spin in the limousine,
enduring the snooty stares at stoplights from people in normal cars
who think you're a lowly chauffeur sporting about in the boss's rig.

Or maybe coming home that night
your headlights catch the eyes of a cat working the roadside:
it panics, running a path
diagonal across the road, under your front tire.

At midnight there's no finding an owner,
no one to comfort and thus make yourself feel better,
the teary master in a nightshirt telling you between sobs,
"It was only a cat."

Arriving home you slump from the vehicle
and feel your way in the dark.
You know the path can swing in front of fortune or misery
or zag between the two a whole life.

That's why I keep my fingers crossed, it's a form of prayer.

HARVEST 2001

Raccoons penetrated with such precision
Not a stalk still stood in the rubble,
Some corn crushed, some stripped or broken,
Just a bite or two gone from the tenderest ears.
I know it was raccoons because, coming home
From Sunday's annual community corn roast
Where my potluck contribution was the butter,
I'd caught them scouting two nights earlier.
At 10 P.M. I saw them in their masks
When I looped my car to let the headlights
Illuminate the scene. A whole damn family
And the mother yawned at me like the yaw of a crane
Eager to pull apart the piles of destruction
She was still planning. What to do?
I chased them up the maple tree,
Laughed at the glowing sway of marbles, unblinking eyes
Reflecting my flashlight from high branches,
Little pairs of stars floating like a butterfly,
Bobbing and weaving like Muhammad
Ali, the little rope-a-dopes on a limb that know
I have no gun and damned if I'd stay up all night
Anyway. So I've always taken my lumps if they come,
Plant late and hope they discover the neighbors' corn
When it ripens mid-August, I can wait
For September, hope they're habituated
To gardens across the road. But see them
Or a taste of their damage: that's a sign
The corn is close to ripe and any night they'll take
The first good ear, then sample all the rest.
No fence that lets in sun will keep them out,
So of course I pick eleven ears and eat each one,
None really ready,
Which is how I manage to eat all eleven.
It's now or never, tonight could be the night.

And come deep morning, the meaninglessness of my work:
Plant a little extra for the wildlife? Give me a break!
I'm refusing to negotiate, they know no reason;
I think of all the lies I've heard about them.
They do not wash their food before they eat.

I'M BACK

Didn't you wonder at last month's Chick Slam
Who that tall bombshell was,
The one with glasses and what seemed like a wig?
About this tall, with a pot-belly?
And you thought I was home lamenting my maleness!

Oh yeah, I'm back.
And I'm back like a toothache at midnight
Going into Sunday, like an aftershock,
The headache that throbs your eyes into pulsing blizzards
The morning after you wowed 'em
        at the cafeteria, hopping onto a table
To toast with champagne the health of mothers everywhere
Before losing your balance and splaying the linoleum
Upon which you then proceeded to puke.
Remember me? I'm back.

But I'm not back to gross you out
With references to slimy sex
Or rats trapped in your dryer's vent pipe,
Decomposing in the heat of summer.
Not going to tell you of sawing through that plastic duct,
As maggots wriggle off soft meat, crumbling to the cellar floor,
Humping each other in the white, lardy pleasure known to maggots only.

Nor am I back to soothe you with the lilt
Of cherubs soft on clouds, the crisp air
Emanating rays of golden sun and green, green grass,
The ocean lapping sandy beach,
A tiny sailboat bobbing on the horizon.

But are you even with me on that boat
When I am gonna let you take the helm
As I tend the sheets and trim the sail?
Take us where you will! There's a sandy beach,
A lovely patch of grass.
We'd have a bit more space
To cast our wishes upon the earth,
To put out each desire like a picnic.

CLICHÉ

When the conference room telephone interrupted the Language
        Arts meeting
we stared at our hands on the tablecloth
our debates now meaningless,
tongues stalled; who can break down

and weep but the one whose son is suddenly taken,
a bad place for bad luck to settle,
like a roulette wheel marble wavering
toward the circling slots.

We wrote our notes, sent flowers:
I guess it helps.

Yet *you* should try coming up with some words
that haven't been said,
some conglomeration of syllables
perhaps with grunts and strange inflection

that haven't been uttered in shock
countless times each day across the world
the marble settled at the center of the spin,
words tumbling out in search of new order.

QUESTION

She's reading in bed, aloud,
a poem by Naomi Shihab Nye,

and he has agreed to listen,
beside her under the covers,
head on his buckwheat pillow
that crunches a bit each time
he moves.

She is puzzling how the man died
in the poem, suddenly, sure.
But by accident, disease
or his own hand? His pillow
crunches as he turns to tell her
whatever she interprets is the answer
is the answer, and he crunches back

to the fetal position, facing the wall,
back curved like an end parenthesis,
his left ear up through which
her words and Naomi's filter,
"What does it mean that
the poem shifts to yet another character,
and that guy's hobby is how the poem ends?"

"How did you choose this poem anyway?"
he yawns, avoiding her question
in obvious annoyance.
The promise of sleep dangles
in his closed eyes, Snowflake Bentley
shapes in antique ivory against a
very dark, blue background.

"Well, it's those lines with the horse,
how it exults in that sound horses make
when they go 'hrumph,' getting everything out.
I love that passage. I want to do that!"

He's brought back from two stars joining.
One floated over the other, superimposed
and was about to turn into a vague sun,
not blinding but very close,
an antique, ivory sun, slowly fading to green,
that predictable final step

that always seems new and is unmemorable
before sleep.
Brought back to "I want to do that!"

And knows, as he mumbles assent, understanding, that exultation
—a fat horse heaving everything out in delight—that inevitably
—a sign of life!—he'll do the old reverse:
inhaling start again to build a new reserve of two stars melting
into one, slowly turning green, like the sun.

SATURDAY

So I'm writing this epic that will change the world
should I decide to make it public
when this crow flies overhead
and seems to hover, which is something I've never seen,
inches from my upturned face
before lifting its black bulk back to the sky.

So I go back to the epic when this car,
a green '43 Buick convertible with the top down,
pulls into my yard and three men in long coats
jump out and call across the yard:
"Are you Geof Hewitt?"
I tell them no and they jump back in the Buick
and roar off. I never see them again.

So I return to my epic poem that will change the world
and I feel my attention's shift like a quick jolt
in the earth's rotation, it's like this
indescribable "What are you doing?"
of the insides of one's body,
bones, guts, even skin and brain asking:
"What *are* you doing?"

And I'm thinking about priorities.
A chocolate would taste pretty good 'bout now.
I've been through a lot, you know,
seen a lot of strange things.

THE BOTTLE OPENER

Tough to be the sideshow in a cheap circus.
I fell in love with the bearded lady, courting patiently,
Wooing, wooing, wooing, until, reluctantly,
Half drunk one night she came into my bed,
Which is when I learned she was a man.

Tough to be the sideshow freak,
The peanut crunching crowd lines up to pay six bits
To watch me do my thing:
I open bottles. I am the magic bottle opener,
The love struck guy with no one on his side

Except the person in the next booth down,
The bearded, so-called "lady." Makes me wish
I'd gone to high school, learned a different trade.
See these scars? The scars above each eye
And below, where most folks carry their bags?

Heroic markings of my work. My vision
Is still good. I can see across the room,
Admire the bearded lady's bust at twenty yards,
But man these scars can burn on sweaty nights!
I don't do no twist-off bottle caps,

But jam the bottle's neck into the socket,
Feel the eyeball pushed back toward the brain,
And slam the eyelid down to grip
The ridges of the rounded cap,
Then jerk upwards on the bottle's base.

It only hurts when beer foams out
Or spits itself into my eye.
Hey, I can do it with my teeth as well,
But anyone, with practice, can do that.

RIGHT AFTER THE INSTITUTE

When I say goodbye to someone I love it feels good, the hug,
And maybe someone's shoulder catches a tear.
I've seen one or two on a hot summer day
Spreading into light cotton blouses and shirts.

What good luck not to start blubbering!
Carried off by the moment, making promises
No sane person could ever keep.
What excuses any sane person can make apply to me.
Your shoulder's wet? That's because I love you.

But don't expect no late night phone calls
Or a postcard asking if you're still doing your life's work.
I guess it's a teacher's lot to say goodbye.
Students make the promises. Stuff like
"I'll write you from college."

Sometimes I worry about those who do. Like,
Get a life and seek new moments of focused community!
You found the Institute, you can find
Or maybe you can found another.

Perhaps you know you'll never hear from me again
Unless you make the effort to reach out.
But you will find replacements who will also mist up
And evaporate at parting. Let 'em go. They were meant
Only for the time you were together. They've got families, too.

Just continue what you did with me,
Let your summer's learning steer you
Through fall and inevitable winter. By then you'll know,
You'll know whether this is really for you.
And if it is, don't let anyone ever tell you "No."

While we are on the subject, remember your peers:
They can be the geniuses of your life.
That kid you met at the Institute can be your lifelong friend,
Someone to outlast your teachers,
Who have no wish to break your heart.

SEPTEMBER WALK

Humming from the lake, not mosquitoes
but those jet skis where the person stands:
A modern miracle! I can walk on . . .
but the big grin and yell disappear. If he'd
only been looking where he was going, the pier
didn't budge and, to help us feel better,
the doctor said he never knew he was dead.

You think I make this up for the cheap burlesque?
Do I even wonder whether I'm inventing it?
Answer: no. It comes from a higher power,
a gift that flows *through*, as Colin said,
"When all the ducks are in a row." It's not
your everyday occurrence like when you read in the paper
someone you didn't know has hit the pier

or is circling the drain, as the British doctors say
when the patient is not expected to last
through the next pay period. It's a crime
we have to laugh to make ourselves feel better
when, after all, we didn't exactly *ask* to be here in the first place.
A little late night fun or an unexpected quickie
and you are summoned, then become attached
through suffocating months before bursting
out to breathe, to walk with the moon
to your back and step on the shadows of your feet, watching Mars
begin to tire of its ascent.

Don't ask the Martians what they want,
or if *they* chose to exist. We thought them up,
poor things, not likely joviated through tickling and lusty pleasure,
but creatures of imagination and thus too real to contemplate.
We're the only ones: God told us so.

Turning as the asphalt path becomes the parking lot,
I walked backwards in the fresh, empty space,
eyes square on the man who, in spite of being called "the moon,"
has never shown his backside. He's done a month's duty
as long as history, year after year, keeping inconstant but reliable watch
on us, a servant of sorts, especially to lovers

who find excuse in his majesty to behave like bunnies.
I shifted focus to the lake and saw how deep still water
holds the clouds, the sky, the moon,
and Mars, in spite of itself, ascending deeper.

PENCILS

Whenever I hold a pencil, its narrow hexagon of hope
Pressing a red rectangle into my middle finger,
I think of my third grade teacher
All three years I was in third grade,
Old Miss Auld, the queen of repetition,
Each year the same, The Lesson Plan
The same each year.

First Monday in October
She finally got out our pencils for the year
And showed us the box, then gave her unit
On pencil sharpening, demonstrating generously
On the shiny chrome grinder screwed to the molding
Of the corner closet. Tuesday
She reviewed Monday's unit, grinding again,
And showed us the various ways of holding a pencil
On her overheads which now,
I am told, she has subsequently converted to Power Point.

Come Wednesday she reviewed
Unit One and Unit Two,
Adding a comment or two
About the penmanship displayed
Below the pencil clutching finger styles
Projected again on the roll down screen
She always asked Robert Kerr to set up and take down.

By then we were salivating for a pencil to hold,
Almost horny to write,
But Thursday she still dangled the eight inch promise
Of our own, bright yellow, Number Two
Wooden writing stick,
Unveiling again the box

From which our pencils would emanate,
Fondling one throughout Thursday's unit
On the appreciation of simplicity.

Friday would be the day
—if we were good—
We could each have our own,
Our sword of thought
With which we soon enough would be skewered
Like butterflies pinned to the display board
In the Science Lab
As, come Halloween, she told us to write our reports,
And every day revise them for the next two weeks,
Then what we were hoping to get for Christmas and why.

A new assignment every second Monday,
The same assignment every second Monday,
The same assignment every second Monday, every year.

TESTING

I went to test the ice, *is it still slippery?*
I wondered, shifting booted feet upon the glaze.
My legs went up, whole body parallel
to the surface reaching up to greet my head.

Some test! Almost like the one my mother-in-law
exacted on the kitchen cleaner, choking down
what she had seen her daughter, then a toddler,
gulp in young anticipation of a green syrup,

maybe sweet until her tastebuds answered,
two or three swallowings late for sure,
that she should drink no more. Having seen the girl
(the woman who became my wife) grimacing and tearful,

detergent bottle on the kitchen floor, Momsy
had to see if it was poison, drained the bottle and waited.

This is how we fools endure the sense that no one
needs to suffer more than we: we test the ice and fall,

we bonk our heads in proving we were right:
Yes! Steer clear of that patch. It's treacherous and slick.

The proof would have rested on the kitchen floor,
mother and daughter dead or comatose at least,
green bubbles, soapy froth, emerging from their mouths,
waiting for Merton, back from barnyard chores, to call the doctor.

An antidote, perhaps too late to work: *Walk them!*
slumped like midnight drunks, across the floor and back
repeatedly until their legs no longer drag and they
are keeping step, maybe even murmuring their names,

a slow recovery, but soon enough they'll
regain appetite for something sweet: *Just don't make it green!*

The man whose lessons learned come slow, mounting his feet
from the ice, places one foot firmly on the glare, rises enough
to get the other foot in place, then steps away and: *Whomp!*
He's on his ass again, laughing through the grimace
            at his foolishness.

My father told of a fellow student, undergraduate days,
testing motorcycle on its back, drive wheel whirring,
loses a finger in the spokes, too shocked to shut the engine down,
sits studying his red stump. Someone happens by and yells

over coughing engine, through blue smoke:
How did you do that? The student looks up calmly,
inserts another finger in the blur: *Like this.*
And blood flies everywhere.

WHEN YOU GET TO BE MY AGE

You think you can get away with anything.
Cop stops you driving the wrong way
On a one-way street, you look at her with the confusion and lust
That only an old man might muster at the same time
And smile apologetically, looking deep into her baby brown eyes:

"What seems to be the problem, Sir?
Have I done something wrong?"

When you get to be my age
These screw-ups happen all the time.
The egg carton stored safely in the oven
With its cradles of eggs, the pot roast squeezed
Into the dairy bin of the fridge
And you're proud to have remembered to turn the oven on
And set to "Bake" level at four hundred degrees.
Until you hear what sounds like popcorn,

Those crazy, exploding jumbos shooting their shells
Into the protective armor of their carton.
Ah, when you get to be my age,
You're looking for your own crate,
One that'll hold you securely as eggs, but big enough
No one's gonna bake you in it.
When you get to be my age
Life ain't so bad except that it happened too fast.

J-A

When my dear friend died, she called to tell me
She'd blown smoke into his face, dabbed whiskey
To his lips, both pleasures he'd been forced to quit
Under her perhaps relenting eye these last twenty years or so.

It's that she's Irish, knows the blur a little whiskey brings,
And what's a drink without a good smoke, something that declares
This is the moment, highlighted by these guilty pleasures,
Another will harvest even more: Who's driving?

And she'd have danced at the funeral or, in her words,
"Cast myself, a grieving Irish widow, screaming into the open pit."
And of course we understood. But dancing? Why not?
Don't give me any of that "This is what he would have wanted" stuff.

Who needs that excuse? Just get your body moving,
Splash some whiskey on our lips, blow a little smoke our way.

THE PERFECT HEART

Scouring the beach for stones tumbled smooth,
He also looks for those in the shape of a Valentine.
So many triangles! But most without the divot up top
And rounded shoulders funneling down to a point,
The perfect heart.

He gathers all potential runners-up,
Maybe twenty or thirty that in a pinch could pass
For love tokens. But underneath seas' clutter
The perfect heart awaits uncovering,
Another tide, another season, another year.

He shares the take with his wife, who spies the least likely,
Damaged and cockeyed like a child abused by birth,
A rough approximation of what one might select,
Proclaiming it the one she thinks will pass.

Who can forecast the choice of one with whom
One has spent more than half a lifetime,
Who can know another's standards for the perfect heart?

ABOUT THE AUTHOR

Geof Hewitt grew up in New Jersey and graduated from Cornell University in 1966. After earning two advanced degrees and teaching for a year at the University of Hawaii, he moved to Vermont and soon met Janet Lind, who grew up on an Iowa farm and was traveling through the area. They married, and a couple of years after their son Ben was born they moved from the relative luxury of their nineteenth-century farmhouse to a small cabin that, without electricity or running water, they'd built with the help of friends. Janet milked cows on a neighbor's farm; Geof wrote his poems and earned a subsistence living as a freelance writer, editor, and occasional writer-in-the-schools.

In 1975 Rodale Press commissioned Geof to travel the country, interviewing self-employed people. Shortly after *Working for Yourself* was published, he took a job with the state arts council, and the family moved to Calais, Vermont, where Ben's sister Anna was born. Geof left the arts council in 1988, and within a few months found work as a writing consultant for the Vermont Department of Education, a position he held until 2009, when he turned sixty-six. He still teaches as a visiting writer-in-the-schools and for an undergraduate B.A. program for adults.

Since 2000, Geof has been active in poetry slams, either competing or hosting. In 2004 he won the Vermont slam championship and, because no sanctioned championship has been held since, he continues to boast that he is the state's "reigning slam champ."

OTHER RECENT TITLES FROM MAYAPPLE PRESS:

Don Cellini, *Translate into English*, 2010
    Paper, 70 pp, $14.95 plus s&h
    ISBN 978-0932412-911

Susan Slaviero, *Cyborgia*, 2010
    Paper, 78 pp, $14.95 plus s&h
    ISBN 978-0932412-904

Myra Sklarew, *Harmless*, 2010
    Paper, 92 pp, $15.95 plus s&h
    ISBN 978-0932412-898

William Heyen, *The Angel Voices*, 2010
    Paper, 66 pp, $14.95 plus s&h
    ISBN 978-0932412-881

Robin Chapman and Jeri McCormick, eds, *Love Over 60: an anthology of women's poems*, 2010
    Paper, 124 pp, $16.95 plus s&h
    ISBN 978-0932412-874

Betsy Johnson-Miller, *Rain When You Want Rain*, 2010
    Paper, 74 pp, $14.95 plus s&h
    ISBN 978-0932412-867

Geraldine Zetzel, *Mapping the Sands*, 2010
    Paper, 76 pp, $14.95 plus s&h
    ISBN 978-0932412-850

Penelope Scambly Schott, *Six Lips*, 2010
    Paper, 88 pp, $15.95 plus s&h
    ISBN 978-0932412-843

Toni Mergentime Levi, *Watching Mother Disappear*, 2009
    Paper, 90 pp, $15.95 plus s&h
    ISBN 978-0932412-836

Conrad Hilberry and Jane Hilberry, *This Awkward Art*, 2009
    Paper, 58 pp, $13.95 plus s&h
    ISBN 978-0932412-829

Chris Green, *Epiphany School*, 2009
    Paper, 66 pp, $14.95 plus s&h
    ISBN 978-0932412-805

Mary Alexandra Agner, *The Doors of the Body*, 2009
    Paper, 36 pp, $12.95 plus s&h
    ISBN 978-0932412-799

For a complete catalog of Mayapple Press publications, please visit our website at *www.mayapplepress.com*. Books can be ordered direct from our website with secure on-line payment using PayPal, or by mail (check or money order). Or order through your local bookseller.